BEING DEAD

I don't know if I'd pin one genre label to Rich's writing. His work is daring and inventive literary fiction, with mainstream appeal. His tone is introspective, mysterious, beguiling, dark, humorous, composed, yet provocative.
—John McManus, Whiting Award Recipient and Author of Fox Tooth Heart

Like that of Don DeLillo or Joy Williams, the work of Richard Leise hums with mystery and an almost cosmic kind of power. With a sincerity rarely found in contemporary literature, Leise explores the mysteries of the human experience in an increasingly uncanny world. He does this in exquisitely crafted, winding sentences that can encompass whole lives or spiral into the deepest moments of personal revelation. This is writing that lets the numinous shine through the seams of the everyday, writing that reveals to us secrets we never knew we had.
—Kent Wascom, Author of The New Inheritors

Being Dead

by Richard Leise

Being Dead

Edited by Carrie Allison-Rolling

Proofed and formatted by Stephanie Ellis

Cover illustration and design by Elizabeth Leggett

First Edition: September 2023

ISBN (paperback): 978-1-957537-79-5

ISBN (ebook): 978-1-957537-78-8

Library of Congress Control Number: 2023945141

BRIGIDS GATE PRESS

Bucyrus, Kansas

www.brigidsgatepress.com

Printed in the United States of America

For Adelle.

Content warnings are provided at the end of this book

AUGUST 10, 1983

Jude wasn't surprised that the doctors caught on. What he couldn't believe was how long it had taken them to figure out he was faking. While the situation didn't look good—Mary, his sister, admitted this freely—she also told him to be strong, because this, like anything, was an incredible opportunity. Jude wasn't so sure. Reclining, for what would be the last time in his hospital bed, Nickelodeon bright on the wall-mounted TV, Jude said, "How?"

Ready to wait for a reply—Mary was slow to speak—he unwrapped and popped a cherry Luden's into his mouth (a necessary habit because his throat was always dry from not talking), careful to place the unfinished lozenge on a napkin once he had worked up enough saliva. While he trusted his sister completely, he could tell by the way everyone was acting that something had changed, and he was worried, convinced that everything was awful, and that anything he did would end terribly.

For instance.

His parents, those benevolent Bendzes? Well, before leaving for the evening, each had kissed him on the forehead (as they always did), and both had told him to get better (as they always did), only Mother had acted particularly strange. Her movements were routine, perfunctory, lacking emotion and sincerity. Jude easily identified what was different.

She wasn't pretending to be happy.

And there were his nurses.

Their behavior was the most frightening. For months they had been kind and good, and pretty—beautiful, even. These were young women, bright in their tight, floral-patterned scrubs, for whom Jude had developed a genuine sort of adoration. Once the novelty of isolation had worn off, and he no longer received vases of flowers from the parishioners at Our Lady of the Lake, yellow, smiley-face mylar balloons from Mother's childhood friends, or cards from his classmates (certainly their teacher, Mrs. Cooney, had forced the kids to write, but still …), his nurses took notice and brightened his room with personal effects: bringing in balloons when there were none, carnations in bud vases when the other flowers had faded, and drawings and paintings their own children had created.

Jude loved the pictures most, and, from the dresser beside his hospital bed, freed his colored pencils, drawing himself into wild forests, strange scenes he couldn't quite comprehend robots in laboratories? dinosaurs at the zoo? or, thrillingly, attaching himself to smiling, stick figure families. Of course he didn't belong in any of these drawings. Mother and Father owned him until he was eighteen. But, like Father Hours always said, When in heaven, why bother looking down on reality?

Today, though, the nurses were … different. Angry wasn't the right word, and they certainly hadn't been mean. It was just that they acted more like doctors, distant and detached, as if (like the doctors), they did not care about the answers to the questions they were going to ask. Opening his door while knocking (like the doctors), they said "Hi," checked his vitals, and went through the motions of offering him breakfast and lunch. As if he were Mary, they moved around the room like he wasn't there.

For the first time Jude was aware of wasting their time. Ears hot, flushed with shame, he spoke softly, instead of smiling and chatting about nothing. How foolish to think he could create some new normal. Consciousness crashing, he wanted to tear down the drawings he had taped to his walls. He wanted to disappear. Quickly, the nurses atoned. Sure, Jude was a liar, but he was only nine, and a genuinely sweet kid, so something must be the matter. Yet the way they reversed their behavior, suddenly all smiles and hands tousling his hair, left Jude jumpy, wanting to speak with his sister.

Mary, standing in a corner, didn't look nervous—she never appeared anything other than somber—but she was concerned. There had been plenty of opportunities for the siblings to talk, but she kept disappearing, following Mother and Father whenever they left the room to speak with a doctor, or one of the specialists. This left Jude frightened and clueless, running through worst-case scenarios. He was exhausted.

His older sister by two minutes and eleven seconds, Mary had died eight months ago—a freak accident—and Jude was careful not to look in her direction when anyone was around, and he made sure to whisper when they spoke. During her first visit (the same night following the Freak Accident, when Jude, unable to sleep, sat on the sofa, staring at the television), she warned, once certain that Mother and Father were out of earshot, that he was too old to have imaginary friends. She cautioned that, if anyone overheard him talking, especially Mother and Father, they would think he was talking to a made-up version of her, and that he was sick in the head. And no one, she added—at least no one Mother and Father hung out with—believed in ghosts. Unless you believed in the Holy Ghost. So, if you go on telling them about—

"How what?" Mary said, finally answering Jude's question. "To be strong? Or how this is an incredible opportunity?"

Jude retraced his thoughts. Living here, while pleasant, even fun, was little more than self-preservation; he felt as if he were an insect trapped in amber. Then he remembered. He had asked Mary how getting caught, how the doctor figuring out he was faking, was a good thing.

"Both," Jude said, grabbing the cord tethered to the giant remote, and turning up the television's volume. He arranged his pillows and straightened himself. There was still a part of him that believed there must be others who could hear Mary—no matter what she said—and if they did, she would disappear forever.

Mary had no interest in television, but she understood that her brother, given his condition, needed diversions. He was watching Finders Keepers. The "Hidden Picture" round was over, and they were on to Jude's favorite part of the show: "The House." The boys and the girls competing on the blue and red teams searched for an oversized dog bone. Some of the rooms were normal, like his room at Mother and Father's house—which was where they were going to send him—and others were crazy, all dead-ends and obtuse angles, zigzag paint jobs and swirling optical illusions, everything reflecting from floor-length mirrors, spaces designed to confuse the contestants.

Jude longed to live in this room until he was old enough to leave for college, or get an apartment. Other than his IV and bedside table, there was only medical equipment. This had been wheeled into a corner and was blocked from view by his bathroom, a great floor-to-ceiling chamber with a huge wooden door that extended into the room. Like a loft—beneath four wooden cabinets, there was even a sink and mini-fridge—the space was large and clean. A tinted window overlooked a small grass park, its playground abutting a busy street backed by a pretty row of brightly painted houses. High above him, the drop ceiling, its panels painted a soft yellow, was dotted with twenty recessed lights. Jude had counted. When used, which was not often, they provided the illusion of a honeycomb; an effect heightened when the room's lighting, emitted from a series of long panels running horizontally a foot above the floorboards, was turned on. Chilly, the room smelled like outer space. Or so Jude told Mary.

Living here wasn't an option, and every day the doctors worked to evict him. Mary seemed to be saying this was happening. After being discharged from Endwell Memorial, and sent here, to Endwell Children's Hospital, their plan had been for Jude to remain for as long as possible. Once caught—which was to say once one of these doctors came up with a "cure"—Mary would decide what to do. How best to stay safe. A draft crossed the room. The flesh on his arms prickled. His ears ached. Jude slid deeper beneath the covers.

The problem with keeping Jude in place (which was to say attached to Mother and Father), was that everyone believed Mother and considered her innocent. Even Father. Even Jude, himself, was confused. Mary had promised that Father had nothing to do with the Freak Accident, and that Mother was a murderer who had lied to save her own skin. He didn't totally believe her.

"The answer is actually one and the same," Mary said. "You have to make yourself puke again."

Mary didn't smile, but had Jude heard a smile, a faint echo of humanity?

Unlikely.

Tall—Jude had been born the runt—Mary's curly brown hair fell to her shoulders, but she was no longer pretty. That part of her had died. Her face was frozen, her eyes unblinking, locked in an icy stare. White as a baby tooth, she seemed to glow. And the way she moved? Well, she didn't … at least not really. Stiff as a cardboard cutout, she slid, as if pushed. Not a constant presence, she was not a force he could summon, either. When appearing she slowly materialized, as when a television, turned on, "comes together" to inform a full picture. When she vanished, it was the same process, only reversed, Mary a water stain on a piece of paper, drying, until all that remained, like a wrinkle upon time's fabric, was an impression of the space she last occupied. Eventually, this, too, disappeared.

While arms and legs, elbows and knees were prominent if Jude looked hard enough, she didn't appear to be dressed in anything other than a long white robe, and this the shade of a stored lightbulb. Jude was accustomed to her appearance, but if anyone else saw her? They would scream, realizing they'd just seen a ghost.

"Puke?" Jude said. "Puke what?"

He hadn't been startled in a long time, and the sensation was strange. He was no longer medicated—at least he didn't think so—and, unless he was wheeled somewhere for testing, his days assumed the pleasant shape of the boxes on the calendar positioned beside his bed. The idea—one of the doctor's—was that a mental image of time's passage would help ground him, and, theoretically, make him aware of the dangers associated with not eating. Because it was a subliminal, as opposed to a drastic measure, Mother agreed.

Jude had no interest in action. His emotions were like the blank, square spaces contained beneath each number denoting the date—a pleasant, noncommittal, nothingness. He never grew bored, and, when unable to watch one of his favorite programs—the nurses didn't let him watch TV all day—Jude could stare at a square until he fell into a pleasant, hazy complacency. He did miss reading. But Mary insisted he show no interest in anything, and to tell the doctors that sentences made no sense, that a book's pages were like puzzles he could not put together. Jude adapted, spending hours daydreaming long, wild versions of his life, a blend of memories from before the Freak Accident, colored with features from his favorite television shows.

The doctor, a fat man with dirty glasses and a beard—Jude hadn't seen him in months—also deemed it important that Jude be an "agent" when it came to selecting his calendar. Jude could walk, but, because he remained undiagnosed, he had been semi-quarantined. One of his nurses, after visiting hours, had directed him from bed and into his wheelchair, unnecessarily pushing him to the gift shop. The store, surprisingly well-lit, was near reception. The hospital's automatic doors slid open, and a custodian wheeling a trashcan entered the building. It was drizzling, and a warm breeze funneled through the foyer, the smell of wet asphalt raising gooseflesh on Jude's arms and setting his stomach to swirling.

"It's closed, so I can't let you inside," she said, tapping the glass. "But do you see a calendar? One you like more than the others?"

Jude wasn't a … well, he didn't have the medical word for it: Depressed? Crazy?

Moot point. It didn't matter. What Jude wasn't was indifferent. If some doctor was going to make him use wall space for a calendar, instead of one of his collaborative pictures, of course he was going to choose one of the calendars he liked. But Mary, standing behind the nurse, bright, and Word document white, disapproved of enthusiasm. Jude shrugged and pointed to the calendar with a kitten on the cover. He hated dogs.

It was the end of April when he got the calendar, which meant that he had studied—it was his responsibility to flip the pages—five cats. August featured a Bengal, a beautiful animal with cool stripes, black dots, bright green eyes, and oversized, pointy ears. It was fun imagining being a cat, leaping impossible heights, walking the ledge outside his window, traffic passing far below, completely unafraid, interested only in adventure. But imagining and feeling were not the same thing. He could never imagine being Mary. And he could never love a cat, even if he imagined that the cat was himself.

"They're going to feed you," Mary said.

"Feed me? But I don't eat."

Mary waited. She was disappointed. Mary knew just about everything, and she didn't need Jude interrupting.

"Okay," he said. "Listening." He toyed with the tape atop his hand, applied to secure his IV in place, and traced the orange outline left by iodine.

"Everything is different. The specialist has not only asked after you, but he has required each of your nurses to complete paperwork. These are professionals, Jude." Mary faded. Then returned. "They like you, but they are not your friends. The doctors asked Mother and Father what your favorite foods were and …"

Jude thought Mary's memory worked differently than it used to. Before the Freak Accident, she spoke quickly, often without regard to who was listening. Now, she seemed to deliberate before speaking, willfully assembling her memories, then carefully weighing her words. This made Jude uneasy. He had asked Mary about this. She, as usual, answered indirectly, saying that people, the living ones, would be happier if their memories worked this way, too. Everyone—including Jude, himself—spoke without thinking. This made for many mistakes. Mary was so much better at so many things than other people.

"They asked Mother and Father what your favorite foods were before you stopped eating. Father did not know at first, but Mother said key lime pie, vanilla ice cream, Bud's pizza, Sal's meatballs, and Frosted Flakes. And then Father said, 'Iced Animal cookies and Pringles.'"

"Iced Animals and Pringles? But wasn't that you?"

"Obviously he got all weird. Coughed. Cleared his throat instead of speaking. Mother corrected him. Sort of."

Mary drifted. Jude waited.

"Tonight, once you fall asleep, they are going to wake you, once an hour. They are going to make you eat. Then they are going to let you fall back to sleep. An hour later, they are going to bring in more, different food. And so on. At some point they plan to switch to half-hour intervals. Do you understand?"

Jude said he did.

He knew Mary didn't believe him because she kept talking.

"They know you are not anorexic, Jude. The plan they have put in place for tonight? This, they told Mother and Father. This will, once and for all, together with all of the tests, and all of their observations, rule out anything gastrointestinal."

"I don't understand. What 'this'? Food? You mean—"

"Everything okay in there, Mr. Jude?" Kilsa, Jude's favorite nurse, leaned into his room. She was wheeling a monitor down the corridor, and looked busy.

Jude looked at Mary. She nodded.

"Yeah. Why?"

"I thought I heard you talking."

Mary pointed to the television.

"Oh," Jude said. "I guess it was the show."

"That is one crazy game," Kilsa smiled. "Call if you need anything." She indicated the button by Jude's bed. "I'm just down the hall. But you know this. You're a pro by now."

They listened to her walk away. Mary kept talking.

"See?" Mary said. "Things have changed. No one believes you are bulimic, Jude, not in the skinny girl sense.

They have ruled out parasites. They have ruled out cancer. They have ruled out everything, except, with certainty, that you have been making yourself puke. They think you are perfectly healthy.

"Tonight is just a formality. That doctor who made you get the calendar? He is back. He thinks you are reacting to my death negatively. He thinks that you will be too tired to make yourself puke. He thinks that if they feed you when you are very tired, that you will fall back to sleep. That you will not vomit. I agree. I think he is right."

"But I've—"

"It does not matter what you have done. What matters, now, is what you do. They plan to discharge you tomorrow. Let me repeat that, Jude. They are sending you home. Therefore, you must puke. You must prove them wrong. That is what I mean by strong. You cannot fall back to sleep. You may only pretend."

Jude considered Mary's words. He didn't know what to say. He stopped eating because he was tired of puking. It hurt, for one thing, but more than that, he was no longer good at it. There was a time when he could vomit as easily as he could untie his shoelaces. The last few times he tried, it was like his laces were knotted, hopelessly secure, and he simply belched, long, alarming emissions that, eventually, landed him here, quarantined in the psychiatric ward of Endwell Children's Hospital. He followed Mary's instructions and told the doctors that "food hurt," and he refused to eat. Naturally, Mary was right. If they were going to dupe him into eating, puking was the answer, the only viable solution. He just didn't think he could do it.

"You have to, Jude," she said. "Your days of IV living are over."

Back when Mary was alive, she could sense what he was thinking, and this had not changed. If anything, she was more inside his head than before.

"If you do not, they are going to send you home. And you will never, ever, see a room like this again."

"But what if I can't?"

"You must."

"But what if I'm—"

"Then you will never, ever, see a room like this again."

Jude was indebted to Mary for his survival; or, to be more precise, for a certain standard of living. When he thought about it, which wasn't often, he couldn't imagine how his life would have unfolded if she hadn't returned. Christmas night, the car ride home from the hospital, Mother and Father had been emotive as mannequins. Queer shadows cut through the car, shearing their heads and arms at strange angles. The illusion was horrifying. Soft music—Christmas songs—piped through Father's speakers. The sound was absurd, but the alternative—silence—was worse. When Mother and Father were compelled to speak, what one said to another was not meant for Jude to hear, and arrived in the backseat as fractured whispers. Mother wept. Father cleared his throat. Helplessness was already sweeping him away.

Mary made for his bed and stood by his side. Jude liked this. It was as close as they came to physical contact, to holding hands. Even though she was still here, it was as though she wasn't, and he missed her.

Terribly.

DECEMBER 27, 1982

Mary remembered a wonderful PBS special.

A dozen artists were directed to draw, based upon belief or speculation, an alien. The artists had one hour, and worked secretly, in different spaces, off camera. When their time was up, the drawings were set on easels, and the easels placed on four steel risers, the creatures arranged like members of a studio audience. Using a laser pointer to highlight googly single eyes, webbed, amorphous hands, squat bellies, and ears hanging from tentacles, the host asked what each drawing had in common.

Mary had been as delighted as she was stumped.

"Every artist," the host explained, "relied upon human, and animal, attributes." He pointed his space-age laser at nose slits, fingers, pupils, and teeth. "This is because it is impossible to conceive of the inconceivable. Nothing is unprecedented. Nothing is made up. Purely invented. Nothing"—he smiled—"is new under the sun."

Mary didn't understand the program, but she never forgot it, using the lesson as a sort of mathematical proof to help her find solutions when life presented other problems. Now, watching the detectives approach Jude, taking a seat beside him on the sofa, the lesson clicked.

"Hey, Jude," the Tall One said. "I'm Detective Hunsinger, and this," he spoke softly, "is Detective Vossler. Is it okay if we ask you a couple of questions?"

Jude glanced at Mary, who had appeared behind the television. She nodded her head.

He said, "Yes, sir."

"Polite young man," the Other One said. He sat with his knees splayed, forearms on his thighs. He angled his head and smiled at Mother.

Mother and Father stood in the opening separating the kitchen from the dining room. Behind them, the sliding glass door. Through the door, the snow-covered deck. Marked by their footsteps, a section of exposed wood was made greater by the morning's bright winter sun. That place where Mary, the morning of the Freak Accident, had fallen. The spot where Father, on his knees, had dropped to lift her. The trees framing the backyard were more black than green, dark against the thin blue sky.

"More like extremely traumatized." Mother took a step forward. "Is this," and her voice caught. "Is this actually necessary?"

"Yes, Mrs. Bendz," the Other One said. "I'm afraid that it is."

Mother turned to her husband. "James," she said. She opened her mouth. She looked at the detective, then closed it.

Father had shaved. But he looked older. So tired. He had spoken to the police and firefighters on Christmas Day. He had said more words in that one hour than Jude could remember him speaking his entire life. He explained that they never opened presents until after mass. He said he was upstairs shaving, and showering, and had no idea Mary was outside. This was before Mary's first visitation, later that evening, and Jude assumed Father was telling the truth.

Father withheld information from the police, Mary would later explain, but he wasn't responsible for what had happened. He didn't know exactly what Mother had done.

Or had refused to do. No one knew what Mother had done. Or had refused to do. That was why, even though her death was suspicious, it was easy to dismiss what happened as a Freak Accident, and Mother would never be charged with a crime. That was why the detectives, while professionally suspicious, would shrug, and, following her funeral, close the case. Father, Mary maintained, was only guilty of protecting his wife.

Jude protested.

"Even if you saw what happened," Mary had said, "it would be your word against Mother's. They would ask you why you did not tell Father. If you had seen what had happened, and had told Father, none of this would have happened. I would still be alive."

She drifted. And then, "This is not about Father."

Father brought a hand to his mouth and coughed. "Let's let the detectives do their jobs. I'm sure—"

"You're sure? Their jobs? They're detectives. Detectives investigate crimes, criminals. I'm not … whose job is it to …"

The Tall One stood and approached Mother. He didn't look like a TV detective. He didn't look like anyone who went to Our Lady of the Lake, either—those men and women who, Mary had always maintained, were creepy. Those men and women who, while of course not related, looked similar. A bunch of people who, like puppets—like clowns—were always smiling. Speaking softly, a step ahead of her and leaning back his head, his voice was an invisible leash leading Mother towards the stairway. Mother argued, her gestures fierce. Hissing, all but spitting her words, Mother followed him into the foyer.

"Impossible thing, losing a sister. And your twin, as well."

"She's not lost," Jude said. "She's dead."

"Yes. And I'm real sorry about that," the Other One said. "Really. I am. And I'm not here to pretend that I'm going to make you feel better. That's impossible. And I won't tell you I lost a sister, too, because I haven't. That isn't true. But I have been a detective for a long time. I've seen a lot of sadness. A lot of terrible, unfair things that have happened to good people. If your family needs help? If you need help? Well, that's the only reason we're here. To offer assistance. To help. We're all in this toge—"

"Help?" Mother said, moving past the Tall One and stepping in front of the television. "How can you possibly help?"

Incapable of emotion, Mary had wants and desires. When alive, she did what she wanted. Being dead was much different. There were no distractions. Being dead, Mary saw no obstacles. She suffered no resistance. Jude watched her process what was happening.

"Sometimes we don't know, Jude," the Tall One answered, returning to the room. "So that's why we're here, to find out. Ask a few questions. That's all. And then we leave. We go."

"Unless you reach out to us," the Other One said.

"Unless there's something we can do," the Tall One said.

The Tall One made for their Christmas tree. He toed a few of the unopened presents, and he fingered an ornament. Gently. With obvious care. Father had unplugged the lights when they returned from the hospital, but the sun, streaming from the kitchen, illuminated the tinsel and reflected the points of many bulbs. The effect was grotesque. They took a seat on either side of Jude.

"Detectives," Mother said, moving to the sofa. She stood, faced the Other One. "I agree with my husband when it comes to, well, when it comes to just about everything. I'm sure you know what he does for a living, and I'm sure you know that I'm a mere housewife, a woman who volunteers her time at the church. You have your opinions, and I have mine. So you'll have to excuse me if I don't have quite the same reverence for authority as James. You're upsetting my son, and that's unacceptable. If there's something you need to know"—she shot a glance at James—"please, investigate your souls, put yourself in Jude's shoes, for goodness' sake, and ask yourselves if it's absolutely necessary to ascertain whatever information you're hoping to attain this minute. If it is, then please stop with the"—she threw her hands in the air—"platitudes. Get on with it."

"We understand," the Other One said.

"Hey, Jude," the Tall One said. "You were upstairs when your sister was outside?"

He stared at the television. Mary nodded.

"Yes. I was upstairs."

"Getting ready for mass too?" the Other One said.

"Had you already showered?" the Tall One asked.

"This is what you came to find out?" Mother said. She shook her head. "I'm sorry, but I am not going to apologize. I don't understand what you're doing here. Like James, I appreciate all that you do. We donate to the Police Benevolent Society every year! But we told you all that you could possibly need to know. The child just lost—"

"She's not lost," Jude said.

"Did you see the puppy?" the Tall One asked. He was looking at Mother, reading her reaction.

"Please leave," Mother said, quietly. "Please just go. Come back, if you need to. There's definitely a time and a place for everything. I'm not saying there isn't. But this"— she shook her head—"this can't possibly be either."

"No," Jude said.

"No?" the Other One repeated.

"But you heard your sister talking about the puppy."

He looked at Mary. She shook her head.

"No."

"How could he have heard anything?" Mother said. She was crying. She had put on makeup for the meeting, and her face was a mess. "I told you. He told you. Jude was upstairs, with his father. Jude was upstairs with his father! Mary was … Mary was … well, I don't remember what she was doing."

Helen gasped, then quickly composed herself.

"She kept insisting she saw a puppy, and I pointed out the impossibility of it, the improbability of it." She hugged herself, and James placed a hand on her back. "You remember the snow. The storm." Desperate, Mother was cracking. "I promised her we'd have a look outside before we got in the car. We were running late. But she kept insisting. She kept demanding that we put on our boots. I went—"

"So, just being clear, here," the Other One said. He turned. Looked at Jude. "You're sure you were upstairs with your father?"

Mary nodded.

Jude nodded.

"James," Mother said. "I don't understand what they're doing here. Do detectives … do the police send …"

Mother quieted, her expression changing. "Wait a minute," she whispered. And then, "Get up."

The two men considered her.

"Get up," she said.

The detectives pushed up from the sofa. Standing, they straightened their ties. Mother took a seat, put her arm around Jude, and whispered something into his ear. He didn't respond. She kissed him on the temple, and he stood. He walked up the stairs. The living room was quiet. They listened to his footfalls as he walked down the hall, then the click of his bedroom door opening and closing. A snowplow rumbled past the house, its blade screeching as it pushed snow from the road onto the shoulder. The ornaments on the Christmas tree wobbled, bright with reflected light.

Mother crossed her legs and folded her hands atop her lap. "Leave."

"Sure," the Tall One said.

"Okay if we take a quick look out back before we go?" the Other One said.

"James," Mother said.

Father walked the detectives to the front door. Mary followed the men, and stood by her old sneakers and winter boots, listening to the conversation. The detectives spoke loudly, as if hoping Mother was listening. They shook Father's hand. The Tall One gave him his card. The Other One said they'd be in touch if they had any other questions.

Father cleared his throat. He said, "Sure."

He opened the door. And, coughing, he thanked them.

1975 (GENERALLY) AND CHRISTMAS EVE (EXACTLY), 1982

Helen wasn't the sort of woman who exercised her right to vote. Well, not exactly. She left voting, like most decisions, to her husband, James, an IBM executive (defense contractor) with high-level security clearance. What did she know of politics? Did she truly understand anything regarding world affairs? Certainly no more than James knew his way around the kitchen, or how to run a home, that was for sure. My word. Imagine being married to someone and arguing over politics. Helen shuddered. Just dreadful. Every two years, she dutifully followed her husband to the polling station, waited behind him in line, stepped into the booth, consulted an index card, and made the selections she had asked him to write for her. It was the least she could do.

Emerging from the booth, Helen smiled, took her "I Voted" sticker from one of the older women behind the table, and thanked her kindly. She had ordered James to stop at McDonald's before arriving and purchased eight large coffees for the volunteers, one of whom always complimented her for wearing something red, white, and blue. They never failed to notice. How lovely. Smiling, her hand wrapped around her husband's arm, Helen, proud as a patriot, sauntered from the polling station. James drove her home, leaned in for a kiss, and she told him to have a nice day.

Once she had the twins, though, it was easy enough to rationalize that her vote didn't matter—their county always voted Red—and she gave up the business completely. It had always been more for show, which (Helen was equally pleased with her self-awareness) was just one step above silliness, when you thought about it.

Long Island transplants, the couple, less than a year after marrying, had moved from Babylon to Endwell. In part because James had been offered his current position, but primarily because Helen wanted their children to grow up surrounded by trees and streams, instead of freeways and buildings, and had, following their realtor's suggestion, instantly fallen in love with the region. Having long since fallen out with her family—aside from aging, indifferent parents, James, an only child, didn't have any—it wasn't like they were leaving anyone behind. Yes, Helen maintained a few close friendships with childhood friends, and congregants from Our Lady of Sorrows—the parish where she had been baptized, received her First Communion, was confirmed, and married—but Endwell was only four hours "Upstate." They could visit whenever they wanted.

She was four months pregnant.

The hillsides surrounding Endwell are steep, and they rise several hundred feet above downtown's central flats. From points east and west any number of streams flow into Endwell, and many of these streams have cut deep gorges into the Earth. Inside these gorges streams narrow and wide plunge from nickpoints some 215 feet high into pools of water deep and clear, shallow and blue. While scenic, it is this geography that prevents Endwell from lying on a major transportation artery. While beautiful, it is this topography that separates Endwell from the Interstate highway system. ENDWELL, the T-shirts and bumper stickers read. Ten square miles surrounded by reality.

And there was Our Lady of the Lake Roman Catholic Church. What a building! Helen believed in God like so many teens, absent faith, devoid of religion, disturbed by years of television and endless hours of video games, believed only in the self. Products of a new, blasphemous, Icon Age, these kids, incapable of perceiving pathos unless it was produced and packaged as a show, a commercial, something to be consumed, blindly placed their faith in science.

No thank you.

Passing the cathedral, with Cascadilla Lake, brilliant through James's window (its two-foot waves dimpled and cresting to break across the water's surface), she knew they were home. Admittedly, she wasn't a perfect Catholic—she placed, for example, her husband before God—but who was? And what woman, married to such a man, wouldn't? People were so quick to editorialize. To critique. Who, walking the face of God's green Earth, wasn't a contradiction? James, so quiet, and so gentle—he'd become, as predicted, a wonderful father to their children—was her Peter, her rock, a man who could, and would, deliver her from anything.

While Helen could not speak of world religions, and wasn't, unless you knew her, considered charismatic, she understood what she was: a child of Christ. The Holy Spirit burned deep inside her, and when driving past Our Lady of the Lake that first afternoon in Endwell her stomach swirled just as it had when, years earlier, she first kissed James, her very first—and only—crush.

"A co-cathedral, the church is a seat of the Roman Catholic Archdiocese, Our Lady of the Lake—

monumental, distinctly American, an architectural symbol of religious freedom—conforms, as you see, to a Latin cross basilica plan, at once keeping with longstanding traditions of European design, while uniting two distinct elements: a longitudinal axis; and, above this, as if some great golden chalice tapping Eternity Herself, if you'll allow for a bit of poetic license"—Mrs. Kruty laughed, overly pleased—"a great domed space."

Helen didn't know what any of this meant, but she was impressed. Father Hours had been called away, and Mrs. Kruty, the church's secretary, had agreed to step in.

Helen hid her disappointment.

"How far along are you, again, Mrs. Be—" Slowing, aware that Helen couldn't keep up, Mrs. Kruty leaned a hip, wide as a pew, against a pew.

"Bendz," Helen said. "Though please, Mrs. Kruty, call me Helen." She smiled. "I'm past my due date, actually. They keep saying any day now. I'm just so pleased that Jude and Mary will be baptized here. Father Hours, this whole building, it's as though—"

Mrs. Kruty smiled, and said, "I know. Just wait until we visit the tower. There really aren't words. God certainly is great."

"So you've—" Helen stopped. She considered the woman, then said, "Have you been up to the tower often? I was under the impression that it has been under construction. And for some time. As in months. Years, even?"

Mrs. Kruty would not reveal, exactly, how long she had been with the church. As if she were harboring some great secret. Please. It was evident, and this as early as their first couple of meetings, that, for some reason, the woman found Helen a threat.

Well, what of it?

Most did.

Undoubtedly, Mrs. Kruty had served Our Lady of the Lake admirably. Of this, Helen was sure. But it wasn't like she was a vaccine. Some measure put in place to make life better, or to ward off certain dangers. Women like Mrs. Kruty—and Helen, too!—were meant to be, for lack of a better word, used. Helen didn't presume that, with time, she'd become more effective at organizing the church bulletin, or would somehow reinvent Our Lady of the Lake's annual summer bazaar. The idea was absurd. Of course she, too, would eventually prove expendable. Like a coat in a closet she'd gather, just like Mrs. Kruty, dust. In time, she, too, would be passed along, given to the Salvation Army, worn, but serviceable, ready to fulfill her next role. To perform her next duty.

Right now, though? Helen was useful because she was young. Helen was vital not because she preserved ideas, but because she was an agent, capable of action. Every few years, an institution needed a boost. Everybody knew this. The Church had entered an exciting new era. Mrs. Kruty, with all her talk of marble? Well, she was, presently, as useful as a coffin.

"Well," Mrs. Kruty said. "That's not entirely true."

She turned in the direction of the tower, raised a hand, and rather dramatically extended its index finger. "The spiral stairwell? The one that survived the 1917 Fire?"

Helen eyed the woman sideways. The 1917 what?

Mrs. Kruty went on. "That will be here long after we're gone. Which is why I can take you upstairs. We can't really go anywhere, at least not really." She considered Helen's belly. "But you can see the view! That alone is worth the" —she smiled, extra brightly—"exercise." She lifted her hands, and let them fall. Colliding with her considerable thighs, this created a generous thwack! that reverberated throughout the empty cathedral.

"The truth of it is, well, as much as Father doesn't like to admit it, we don't have the money. We hired contractors, and we agreed upon a plan, but then with the economy, well, we—"

"We" had nothing to do with it. Mrs. Kruty played a large part in the day-to-day operations of Our Lady of the Lake, this much was true, but the woman had no say in the decisions driving the Church's financial actions. Like any parish, Our Lady of the Lake operated from a Chart of Accounts, with a governing body overseeing the institution's assets, liabilities, and equity, offset by income and expenses. The economy—Helen had asked James— was fine. The harsh truth was that churches just didn't have much by way of disposable income. Unless the tower presented itself as a hazard, Father Hours (or any priest, for that matter) could only make suggestions. Like a child, he could wish. The fact that the Church didn't hold a fundraiser, James said, meant that the repairs must run into the tens, if not hundreds of thousands of dollars.

"Besides the view," Helen said. "Which I'm certain is lovely. What else is up there? Father mentions the tower so fondly. There must—"

"Oh, it really is remarkable, Helen," she said. "It's like being atop a castle's turret. There is a wonderful stone room. This space, for the most part, is safe. In fact, Father Hours, given that he has some rather important books there, visits the room several times a month. Checks the mouse traps. Makes sure there isn't any moisture. That sort of thing. He—"

"So it's like an office?"

"Yes," Mrs. Kruty said. "You certainly could say that. Although I might use the word study. There is the most wonderful stone altar, built into one of the walls, and comfortable furniture, and a desk, for writing homilies. It's really—"

"I'm not sure I understand, then," Helen said. "Why doesn't—"

"Why doesn't Father just use the space? Well, don't let his passion fool you. He's no longer a young man. And the area isn't insulated. So he'd have to bring up a space heater, for one. Or a fan, at least, come summer. Which would mean running an extension cord, too. It's just the strangest thing, the air up there. But more than this, the area, the entire, well, ceiling, for lack of a better word, isn't insured. It has passed inspection in that when left alone it doesn't present a danger. There isn't any electricity or plumbing. Were Father to injure himself, or to do damage to the building, we wouldn't be protected. And this room, Mrs. Bendz, it's just one small space. Tiny, really. From there you can walk the length of the church, from front to back, and side to side. Go through a doorway, and take a wrong step? Well, you could fall all the way up there"—she pointed above the altar, behind which was a giant Christ pinned to His crucifix—"to …"

She paused for effect. When Helen didn't bite, Mrs. Kruty changed the subject.

"Now, all this here is classic Greek portico—slender Ionic columns, not to be confused with Doric, an easy enough thing to do … which, well, here, this is arranged in what's described as a double hexastyle pattern. You can see, obviously, that the, well I guess you'd call them towers, directly behind them"—she pointed, as if Helen didn't understand English—"you can see how they give rise to an additional pair of cylindrical towers, one of which is the—"

Yes, the church was stunning. Helen was properly amazed. But did such obvious beauty need verbal clarity? Such a thorough explanation? As a matter of fact, Helen was more impressed that Mrs. Kruty (the plump little woman who sat, in the first pew, every Sunday) could emit so many words! Personally, Helen preferred considering the building from the shore, the southern end of

Cascadilla Lake, across the street from where they now stood, clear water lapping the shale beach and the wind rustling the great shoots of the giant willows fronting the water, some so long as to trace patterns in the park's lush, green grass and providing shade for picnics, a point of vantage flattening the curve of the dramatic gorge carved into the hillside backing the cathedral. She didn't need this Mrs. Kruty droning on when she, herself, was capable of absorbing the domes, noting how they were greater in diameter than the drums upon which they sat, their height exceeding their width, and how the bulbous shapes tapered to points—Our Lady of the Lake's main façade—which, depending upon the time of day and cloud cover, offered a glittering, ethereal vision …

"What with the cathedral's exterior being Lewisian gneiss, which, of course I don't expect you to know, Mrs. Bendz, is a thick, marble, quartzite and mica schist completely blasted through. There are few geologists in the state, let alone Endwell University, who are aware that this is actually the result of melted basaltic dykes and granite magma."

"Do we get many tourists, then?" Helen said, affecting interest.

"Oh, I get my share of calls," Mrs. Kruty chuckled. "Believe you me. And you should see these men, too! How, all dressed like that goofy Doctor Who, the Lord humbles them when, awestruck, they don't understand what's directly before them. Can you believe I've had requests for samples? As if I'd allow any of these foolish men to drill into any one of these precious walls. In fact, just last month a …"

Helen didn't know what to make of Mrs. Kruty. She was pleasant enough, and remarkably competent. But she was a lay person, not a nun. Nevertheless, she wore a navy skirt that clung to her calves; a white button up shirt; a faded navy blazer; flesh-colored panty hose; and black, discount sneakers. No makeup. Even her long gray hair fell like a habit. In a word, the woman was silly.

For her part, Helen wore Guess jeans, a maternity blouse from Macy's, and flats. A touch of lipstick and blush. Eyeliner. Behind her ears just a spritz of Charlie, a Christmas present she purchased for herself last year. She disagreed, and vehemently, with prosperity preachers, but James tithed, and Helen volunteered her time. Christ brought out the best in her, and this cathedral, seemingly aglow with the gentle, delicate pink of idealized beauty, like the turn of a snowflake breaking through the atmosphere …

"… classically detailed, a solid, masonry hemisphere of a type pioneered by the French master Philibert Delorme, inner dome—wooden; stolid; double-shelled in its construction—is at once a study of light and an experiment: twenty-four half-visible skylights occupy, I like to think, like so many open eyes, that space high above the cathedral's crossing which—"

It was true. The centralizing effect was amazing, how this worked to contrast her impression standing outside the church against what, in fact, was a linear, oblong building. But again: it was true. Some things—many things—simply were seen to be believed. Oh, how the very worst of this world has been reduced to, and created by, language. The simplest, the most contrived words, clauses, phrases … how these ruin everything, how all of it is artifice, subordinate, some others' (like the Mrs. Kruty's of the world) playthings.

And just think—

What would pass through our minds if not the thoughts of the sounds of words? In what form would thought assume shape?

What an opportunity for beauty! Such an occasion for precision!

Imagine, then, a world where spoken language never evolved. No vocalizations. No birdsong. A planet where feelings are felt and nothing is implied, misconstrued. Relationships, all relationships, reduced to base levels, the ultimate sums of dis- and affection, a plane where nothing is called anything. No coding. No signaling. All there is but giving and taking. Or taking and giving. Oh, but what is this world if not a collection of the things and conditions we learn to live with?

Why not look at a cardinal, or a cathedral, and think, Wow? And then, Amazing.

But this required humility.

A cultivated—if not innate—sort of grace.

And clearly Mrs. Kruty—

Not quite possessing the diction for what she was feeling, Helen suppressed a sigh.

"I am so sorry," Helen said. She had had enough of this woman and, as if in pain, eased into a pew. "But is there any way I could possibly trouble you for a glass of water?"

Mrs. Kruty paled, and, in that moment, Helen realized how much she disliked the woman … how it was that the woman's words, like snowflakes, lost, upon her tongue, all sense of shape and substance. How it was that the woman's words dripped and slowly ran together as if forming, ultimately, icicles of thought. How everything the woman said was pointless, were tangible objects that fell like fangs from her lips, idiotic thought-objects that Helen could rip from her mouth, snap, and grind beneath her feet.

"Oh my," she said, clutching the slender golden crucifix she wore around her neck. "You're not about to … well. Let's see. Do you—"

Helen smiled, flashed her teeth. "No, Mrs. Kruty. Not yet. I'm fine. It's just that when—"

"Don't you say another word," Mrs. Kruty said, turning. "I will be right back, Mrs. Bendz. You just sit there and stay safe! I'm afraid we don't have much in the fridge, at least at the moment. But maybe you'd like some oyster crackers? I believe I saw a bag …"

"No, thank you," Helen said. "Just the water, please, and thank you."

Soon there was silence. And this silence, as if itself an architect, made of the space a great many windows in symmetrical opposition and marvels of glass meticulously, artfully stained, the interior awash in natural light as if abjectly resenting the weight of that darkness carried in upon the whims and wings of the congregation's modern, impenitent parishioners. Directly overhead, surrounding the dome, a complicated system of barrel vaults and shallow, secondary domes, grids of plaster rosettes adorning its coffered ceiling. Helen's mind emptied, thoughts of future encounters with Mrs. Kruty melting to create the pleasant awareness of being. How strange, and how pretty, the points at which questions cease to begin. And the wall's pale yellows, soft blues, light greens, stark reds and rose. Light-colored, the marble flooring, and inlaid with gold wisps, like grace, manifold. After one more look Helen, using the back of a pew to hoist herself up, side-stepped towards the aisle.

Although she wanted to see the view of the lake from the tower with her children inside her, Helen could not wait for the woman. Anyways, who was she kidding? She was tired. She couldn't climb anything. And it wasn't as though they wouldn't be seeing plenty of each other for the …

Mrs. Kruty would understand.

"She'll probably be relieved," Helen muttered, making for her station wagon.

With two fingers in a font of Holy Water, a bang from behind the sacristy startled her. Making the sign of the cross, Helen made her escape, hand on her belly as she passed through, as quickly as possible, the cool, dim narthex, pushing open one of the building's huge wooden doors, and, back to the railing, crab walking the wide, stone steps to the street.

One major difference between Endwell and Babylon was the temperature. Come four o'clock, Christmas Eve, the mercury had dipped below ten degrees. The sun was setting and it was overcast. Shadows masked rooftops. The gold lights framing storefronts, and the white lights strung from invisible wires overhead, made iridescent the snow, which, thick as Mary's index finger, rose from the branches of those trees planted between Endwell Common's tall buildings.

Helen had been in Endwell less than a decade, but lived like a native. She loved the Commons, which, in addition to Our Lady of the Lake, and Cascadilla Park, made downtown Endwell a destination, somewhere wonderful to visit. Beautiful stone buildings edged what amounted to eight pedestrian blocks, and then the shopfronts themselves, those sutured brick and cement structures, interrupted only occasionally by narrow alleys and passageways. The buildings rose impassively, as if erected to frame the city's glass storefronts and enclose the space. Under winter's fallen snow? Nothing by way of mystery. All was pretty, glazed with a heavenly, earthbound, grace.

Above these shopfronts brick tenements rose four or five stories high, Endwell's expensive apartments and spacious flats, great locations and views, fire escape topiaries, side doors leading to decks enclosed by black, spiral railings, a bit of Manhattan in diorama, and that which made of downtown Endwell the hip place to reside, its youthful, cultural, center. Wind whipped and fell from the sky, a frigid blast. Jude's hat flew from his head. Helen adjusted her scarf.

When Mary was younger, she, too, loved the Commons. Walking atop the cobblestones, studying the sculptures and the fountains, it was as if they lived inside a snow globe, with giant humans observing her family, dreaming (like she did when she held a snow globe) that they could switch places, if only for a day.

Now, Mary, bundled in her Snorkel Parka and Moon Boots, was miserable. It would be one thing if it wasn't freezing. And another if she hadn't been here a million times before. And another if it wasn't Christmas Eve! From the sky and the sidewalk, from flapping awnings and glittering light posts, snow flew sideways, sharp as sand, slashing exposed skin. Bright white and then dark purple, and swollen as a badly sprained ankle, far above Cascadilla Lake, at the north end of the Commons, intracloud lightning illuminated cumulonimbus clouds like the flames of Japanese Lanterns; the accompanying thunder, moments later, was hushed, the storm creating strange, rolling sounds lost in the hiss and the cry of the wind and the driven, swirling snow. This was a weather event, and so the sun, buried beneath a falling atmosphere, made shopfronts mirrors, and apartment windows black apertures opening upon strange worlds. While each realm undoubtedly offered its own sort of misery, each was probably favorable to that, which kids here, on Earth, endured. Mary winced. Pain, like an ice-cold current, shot through her foot.

Naturally, the Commons was deserted. And yes, Helen was a little chilly. But, more than anything, she was exhilarated. James—usually so busy with work—was with them! And secondly … well, why was there always the need for more than one good reason to define something special, let alone a family outing? She had just a bit of last-minute shopping, and then, God-willing, a visit to Our Lady of the Lake to witness the parish's living nativity, an event she played no small part in planning. After that, assuming the children behaved, it was home for hot chocolate and cookies.

"I don't understand why we have to go to church tomorrow," Jude said.

His mom had returned his hat, but had failed to clear the snow. Given the wind, while it was better than no hat at all, the snow, which had frozen atop the fabric, burned his ears. His small face was red and swollen, and white bumps, like bee stings, rose from his cheeks.

"Or why we didn't go to the mall," Mary said. She was limping, and snot ran from her nose.

"Look, Mom"—she pointed to a sign outside Endwell Bank and Trust—"it's two degrees. Two degrees! We could die from frostbite. And look"—she pointed towards the lake, turning her face from the wind—"it's not supposed to thunderstorm in the winter. Is it supposed to thunder in the winter, Dad? And lightning? Can't we just go home? Please?"

Helen ignored them. She was having too much fun to let her children spoil anything. She loved downtown Endwell, the Commons, and both, especially, come Christmas. While Mary had a point, and she empathized, to a degree, James wasn't much of a shopper, so, during the holidays (or before her birthday), Helen purchased what she desired—as opposed to needed—and wrapped the gifts, opening them Christmas morning, affecting some, but not too much, surprise. James's part wasn't complicated. He nodded and smiled.

Of course she wasn't offended!

No one knew the difference. And besides, this was simply part of life in a healthy marriage. For better or worse, both she and James provided, they had their roles, and clearly defined, too. The problem—how stupid of her! —was that with the twins growing older, and becoming more difficult to shop for, she neglected to purchase anything for herself. And there was her work with the church. It was no more her fault than it was James'! But what would the twins think if she had nothing but two presents—the silly little gifts they had bought for her (with her money) from their school's sale—to open, clumsily wrapped, and already, with those gifts that came in the mail, or from her friends at Our Lady of the Lake, beneath the tree?

Besides, it wasn't "two" degrees. The bulbs in that clock had been broken for months, and Mary made that clock read whatever time or temperature she pleased. If it was July, and she was "melting" and wanted to be home, begging to watch TV, she'd say it was 102. Helen stopped in front of a brightly lit storefront. Her family, caught by surprise, collided into each other. They remained huddled for warmth.

Jude was a good boy; he seldom complained. A young Catholic—she had such hopes for him!—his question was a good one. But the mall? Helen considered a black cashmere sweater. Oh yes? Really? So she could get herself a set of steak knives? Or maybe one of those new blenders?

Goodness, and Helen moved on. Mary was growing up to be quite the pest. And suggesting that she was hurt? That she had sprained her ankle?

It was only through the grace of God that Helen didn't turn around and …

She didn't want to confuse Jude, however. Which is why, when James didn't speak, she said, "Oh, hush. It's not that cold."

And then, to Jude, "We're going to mass twice because Christmas is a Holy Day of Obligation." She turned to face Jude, peering into his lowered, frost-swept eyes. "And it's a sin to skip Church on Sunday."

"Then how come we sometimes go on Saturday?"

Helen ignored Mary. She said, "Christmas and Sunday just happen to be back-to-back this year, honey. Personally"— and she leaned into James, deciding against the sweater—"I find it thrilling. If ever there's a time to be thankful, it's now." And then, shouting into the wind-driven snow, "Oh. I think I see a little something ..." and she smiled at her family. "For a certain someone. I. Will. Be. Right. Back."

Careful not to slip, she crossed the cobblestones, wishing a Merry Christmas to the lone couple passing by. She shouldered through a particularly icy wind gust.

Mary, her sore foot throbbing, knew better than to say anything. But, like a prayer, she worked to will want into fruition. And she spit at her mom.

At least with her eyes, anyways.

DECEMBER 25, 1982

Sent outside.

Freezing cold.

Using her hands to mask the glare, Mary stared through the sliding glass doors. The kitchen was dark. The counters had been cleared and scrubbed Ajax clean. She couldn't hear the dishwasher, but Mom had deposited the detergent and closed the door before pushing the button activating the machine, ignoring Mary as she pounded on the glass and screamed, its little green light indicating that it was running. There was no point in shouting, now—everyone was upstairs. Mom had made this so. Mary's eyelashes were frozen. Snot ran from her nose, then iced over. Inside, before the door leading to the garage, a lump of four or five oversized bath towels, dark and swollen with water, the only indication that anything was out of the ordinary.

Pressed against the glass doors, shivering, the snow reached Mary's ankles, her red pajama bottoms frozen to her skin. She could no longer feel her feet. What hurt was her back. Pain moved in lines from her hips to her knees. While she hadn't been outside that long—at least she didn't think so—she was exhausted, and was having trouble standing. Her mom could be so unfair. She hadn't even done anything!

Close to the surface it wasn't that windy. But above Mary, from the rooftop and the chimney, waves of frosty snow particles, white, but sometimes blue, dipped and danced across her heavy, eyelid-shrouded lines of vision. Bold, post-impressionist strokes. Even the breeze in outline.

Mary heard the strange, hushed echo rising from the freshly fallen snow. This is because snow isn't rain. This is because snow, at least not really, doesn't "fall." Snowflakes swirl. A snowflake doesn't cut across the wind; rather, a snowflake is carried by wind's whim.

Snowflakes, when landing on Mary's exposed skin, needled.

Silently, like one thousand tiny fires, these snowflakes burned.

But Mary was freezing. She should be doing, not thinking.

Mary pounded the glass with her fists; she banged the door with her forehead—if only to keep warm. Was there something to break the glass?

Unlikely.

The deck had been cleared before Thanksgiving (not that she could see anything other than snow), which meant the grill and patio set were secure in the garage. And their little backyard forest was too far away to explore. Feet of snow buried the ground. And the branches of the trees and the power lines running to the side of their house were swollen with snow. Great wind gusts blew large drifts from the power lines, from the limbs of trees. Huge shelves of snow falling and whose sounds were swallowed by the last few hours of the storm. Mary covered her ears with her hands, her wet hair frozen in strands thick as icicles.

Not that she would ever act.

Doing something like busting the door would get her grounded through summer vacation.

Frustrated, she would have cried, but she was too tired. Besides, she was wet enough. She didn't think her face could handle two more tears. Mom had her ways, and she stuck to them. Talking back—allegedly—is what got her sprayed with water from the sink, and soaked, and sent outside in the first place.

No sense getting upset.

And there was no walking around the side of the house, either.

Their home was huge, the walk was too long, and the snow was too deep. She'd lose one, or both, of her slippers and socks. That, or she'd fall, and get stuck, lost until Mom sent Dad to dig her out.

Besides, Mom had said to stay put until she cooled down. So it wasn't like she would let anyone get the door if she rang the bell, anyways.

She was in timeout.

And Mom was a broken clock.

JANUARY 1 – 9, 1983

In the days and weeks following what The Endwell Standard called a Freak Accident (the headline running above the fold), Jude did not experience shock, denial, guilt or anger, entering directly into depression, a depth of mourning incomprehensible and heavy as a lead apron. He hurt. His ribs, his kidneys, his skin ached as if for a want of movement. The terror. The fear that he was going to do something terrible. This arrived later.

Reality was even worse, walking a cruel exercise in agony, his feet sledgehammers all but impossible to lift, each successive footfall percussive, the sensation shaking his skull and rattling his teeth. Sitting might have been worse. Motionless, he felt pitched forward, perpetually resisting some phantom hand clutching his shirt and dragging him, face first, to the ground. And should grace ascend and he happen to escape thought? This was not much of a favor. For, when, the result of some sound or sensation, Jude was jolted out of what passed for reverie to realize the horror of his situation, he'd wheel about as if weightless, jerking, arms outstretched and overcorrecting.

It wasn't so much that Jude wanted to die.

He simply found living too challenging.

Waking up was the worst. Heart racing from whatever bad dream he'd been having, sound was too loud. The world was too bright. Then he would have to get dressed. Coursing through his consciousness the feeling, like a current, that he was not quite in control. That not only did he hurt, but that he might …

And then there were visitors. Casseroles and dry kisses. Everyone smiled and was nice—even the ladies Mother disliked. But their comments felt like challenges, minor insults, as if the women were egging him on and wanted Jude to crack, to push back. As if he owed them a reaction.

"I'd say not just yet," Dr. Greene advised, when Helen called, wondering if she should bring Jude in. "Let's give it a bit of time."

The twin's pediatrician since infancy, Dr. Greene had, after reading the story in the paper, immediately called Helen. No one picked up, and he left a message. He had expected a call, but, upon hearing Helen's voice, was surprised to feel so much emotion. Having never lost a patient so suddenly, he remained heartsick. Stunned. Mary, so headstrong, had been such a wonderful child. And Jude. What was there to say about Jude?

"But what about church? What about school?"

Helen wept. Her words arrived separately, garbled pleas and jagged shouts.

"It's like he's no longer here, with us. It would be different if he were crying, or, well, anything. But he just sits, and stares. Sometimes," Helen lowered her voice, she spoke as if she were ashamed. "Sometimes I catch him talking to himself."

This interested the doctor. "Regularly?"

"Regularly? What do you mean? Do you mean every day? All day? It's bad, though, right? Who knows what he does when I'm not around. What? Are you worried? Should I bring him in? Because I—"

"Helen," Dr. Green said. "You're reading far too much into this … Which, by the way, is fine. Completely understandable. I'm simply asking as Jude's doctor. How about—"

"I'm really worried, Doctor. Really and truly. It's like he's listening, too. Not just talking but listening to someone who isn't there! I know I don't need to tell you, but Mary was his world. I don't think I know how to help him."

Until the Freak Accident, Helen had lived a charmed existence. A decent woman, Dr. Greene found she straddled the line between happiness and arrogance. At times overbearing—he knew how she mothered—Dr. Greene loved her children. And so, by extension, he found Helen tolerable.

"Grief is impossible to predict, Helen. For now, as upsetting as I'm sure this is, this is Jude's new normal. And, as impossible as it may seem, you must take care of yourself, too. Jude is a wonderful boy. But this …" Dr. Greene used his free hand, as if reaching for the right words. "This is a terrible thing. So, in these trying times, just watch him. Love him. Give him space. But if you are concerned? If you see signs that something truly is the matter? Won't get out of bed? Becomes combative? Doesn't respond when you speak with him. Anything out of the ordinary, Helen. If something comes across as acutely strange? Please. Call me immediately. Straight away. I am here. Any time, night or day. Okay? We're all in this together. These are unchartered waters. And listen. If you want someone to—"

From his seat on the sofa Jude eyed Mary, standing in the kitchen, listening to the conversation. She flickered brightly, before, as Mother, clearly disappointed, hung up. Making an appointment was her way of managing that which couldn't be controlled. Turning her head, Mary studied Jude before fading to nothingness.

Sunday school was the worst. Mary and Jude had never been interested in kids their own age, immature boys and girls whose personalities informed bizarre behaviors that the siblings found boring. The twins were in no hurry to abandon wonder. If anything, the opposite held true, the two inventing their own characters and kingdoms and, however inadvertently, combining their ability to identify patterns, solve problems, and apply logic to basic questions to create one, shared, Supermind. Through a series of simple questions posed to their parents, they eliminated any hope for the existence of such becalming charms as the Tooth Fairy, Santa Claus, or, more ludicrous than anything, the Easter Bunny. They might as well believe in Papa Smurf, they laughed. Not that Mom let them watch television.

And people thought they were strange …

The upshot was that their imaginations had far more room to roam. The downside was that the other seven- and eight-year-olds comprising their First Communion class, while pleasant enough, were insufferable, were utterly reliant on Mrs. Hawke, their "teacher," unable to execute tasks with more than two directions. Respecting rules to so great a degree that even minor deviations in expectations could leave any kid crying, others, so wowed by social stories like "Jonah and the Whale," were, for fear of missing the ending, unwilling to rise from their square floor mats to use the bathroom, and had "accidents."

Our Lady of the Lake, Boys Academy, wasn't much better. Jude did not hate school, but he didn't enjoy it, either, finding it particularly frustrating that he was separated from Mary. While he, like Mary, understood that education was an obligation, nothing worth resisting, he didn't have a favorite class. Happiest at home with Mary, isolated atop the West Hill, the twins spent hours outside exploring, inventing games, becoming, in time, with their inside jokes and shared, cultivated secrets, a force wholly unique, fantastic, and mysterious to others—even their parents.

And they read. They loved the lake. The ocean. The idea of sinking. Of forever falling. Secure in their self-made cocoon, they evolved. Not abnormally. But not exactly normally, either. Like deep-sea creatures evolving not as a result of sunlight's consequence but from that light which they themselves created, they evolved. Like a cloud, Mary might drift or storm, a stimulus affecting their environment, never responding to what the world presented, but, rather, organic and fluid, a solution in search of a problem worth creating. Jude loved little more than standing in the shade of her cast consequences.

School resumed Monday, January 3, ten days after the Freak Accident, and five days following Mary's funeral. New Year's Day, with Father watching football, Mother asked Jude if he had considered returning to school.

Jude lied. He shook his head.

Helen smiled. "It might be good for you. Seeing all your friends, taking your mind off things? Really and truly. It really might do you a world of good."

Quiet, Jude was popular. That he came from money was obvious (never a bad thing), and his aloofness was intoxicating, pegged as a form of coolness his classmates didn't understand yet admired, and tried to imitate. The other boys went out of their way to include him. Indifferent, Jude would join them, even enjoying himself on occasion.

"Do I have to?" Jude asked.

"No," Mother said. "Of course not." She hugged him, then, stepping back, rested her hands on his shoulders, adding, "You don't have to do one single thing until you are absolutely, one-hundred percent, ready."

James, though. Jude's father. He could conceive of no reason to stay home. Why? To be a presence? To give himself more time to grieve? And if he elected not to report Monday, why stop with one day—why not take three? And if he stayed home through Wednesday, why not just go ahead and make it a week?

No.

It didn't add up.

What was the purpose? Jude was a ghost, a kid watching television—a treat, given the circumstance—and eating, with disinterest, what Helen fed him. When, come early afternoon, Helen snapped off the TV and suggested he try reading a book, or work on a drawing, he nodded, responding, if asked a question, with single syllables, retreating further into himself. Helen, while upset, was no longer visibly traumatized, and had, following the funeral, discarded the medication she had been taking since the afternoon of the Freak Accident, and spent her days on the phone with Mrs. Kruty, Father Hours, or some other lady from Our Lady of the Lake.

There was no question, Mary's death altered James. But his little girl was never coming back, and so what was the point in permitting his tragedy to disrupt and inconvenience the lives of dozens of subordinates? What good could possibly come from leaving them feeling uncertain, bracing for the awkward conversations associated with his return? God knew James hated being in even remotely similar positions. And so, to the question of: Name one good reason to stay home? The answer was simple. There wasn't one.

The week passed quietly. While Jude didn't want his parents to disappear completely, and was glad someone was in the house—he knew he could never hurt them—this wasn't because he was lonely and wanted companionship. Ironically, their presence made it possible for him to attain the almost complete isolation he craved. Distance from others did not create pleasure—in Mary's absence, all that remained was pain—but when alone he was less uncomfortable. Seeing Mother or looking upon Father was unpleasant. He suffered a strange, physical reaction, as if he'd been stung, his skin sore and throbbing. With Mother around, but not visible, Jude was responsible for nothing, able to engage loneliness as explorers test levels of self-reliance, searching for ways to lose consciousness. This didn't mean he wanted to die. He believed others when they said that while he would never forget Mary, this pain would pass. Certainly, everything would have been different had Mary left him completely, but she hadn't, and her visitations were thrilling, an antidote for the emptiness of existence. With each apparition Jude, as if blinded and bodiless, aware only of his insular connection with thought, so that even after she, for whatever reason, vanished, Jude sat mesmerized, senseless, momentarily happy. His only concern was what he might do. Within, or absent, her presence.

Jude had never seen Ripley's Believe It Or Not!, but the segment on underwater creatures was unimpressive and easy to believe, the host's playful enthusiasm, like that of Mrs. Cooney's, or any of his former teachers, failing to capture Jude's imagination. A Chinese ritual involving papers, blood, and human tongues was, apparently, utterly "unbelievable," the voiceover, bleeding into and out from every commercial break, suggested, teasing the upcoming content. Jude wasn't holding his breath.

Father, dressed in loafers, slacks, and a sweater, entered the living room from the kitchen. Earlier, when Mother had returned from Our Lady of the Lake (Father attended the eight o'clock service, ensuring Jude wouldn't be home alone), she wondered, aloud, wheeling the vacuum cleaner behind her, if maybe today might be a good time to remove the Christmas tree, given how much it was shedding. She left the machine beside the sofa. Mother had taken down the decorations earlier in the week, had placed the wrapped presents in the back of her station wagon, and had removed the red, knit cover concealing the stand. All that remained was loosening the metal prongs from its trunk, freeing the metal stand, physically removing the tree from the living room, and leaving the husk on the curb for the city to carry away.

No weekend warrior, Father detested manual labor. If he could have hired someone to remove the tree he would have, but he was wise enough to know that completing just enough tasks—like taking their cars for oil changes, and putting his dirty laundry in the hamper—provided the illusion that not only did he work fifty hours a week, he helped around the house, too. Wherever possible, he paid others to carry out necessary work, such as mowing the lawn, or cleaning the gutters. Lost, his expression pained, he considered the tree as if the project were a puzzle. Televised light filled his glasses as the program resumed.

"What is this?"

"Not sure," Jude said.

"That is one tall tower." He cleared his throat.

Jude nodded. He did not like heights.

Father wasn't that annoying. His company wasn't that painful. He didn't want him to, but Jude didn't mind if he stayed. On the television a tall wooden construction rose from a clearing. Around the tower, which, the narrator noted, was assembled for utilitarian purposes, and lacked aesthetic appeal, were tall trees, a canopy like you'd find in a rainforest.

"What did he say? One hundred feet?"

"Yes," Jude said, scratching his neck. If only Father would stop talking, he could stop thinking about falling. Of hurting himself. Or, worse, someone else.

They listened to the host. They watched a group of women in bright colors dancing and singing. Mother was in the laundry room. She closed the dryer door and pushed start, the clothing slowly tumbling, the machine humming. Mother's solution to navigating what she constantly called "these troubled times" was to never stop moving.

"Pentecost Island," Father said. He coughed. "Ever hear of it?"

Jude shook his head.

"It's located in the South Pacific. A place called Vanuatu."

Father was incredibly smart. For years, Mary and Jude had pleaded with him to try out for Jeopardy! He rarely responded, or, if he did, said, "Maybe."

"Only reason I know about it is be—Wow."

A man dressed in what looked like a diaper leapt from the platform. He arced, and then dropped to the ground. The picture was grainy, so it was difficult to see the vines wrapped around the man's ankles. Before the previous commercial break, the program featured the man preparing for the jump, putting certain protections in place, but still, the sight was alarming. The man's arms were crossed before his chest, his head tucked at a strange angle. The vines prevented him from smacking the earth and snapping his neck, and his shoulders barely brushed the forest floor. Men rushed forward to cut him free. Jude, while he believed the man had jumped, was amazed that people could be so stupid and so brave.

Normally, Father would be comfortable in his recliner, drinking a Coke over ice and watching 60 Minutes, Mary and Jude half-heartedly playing Monopoly or War, knowing that, at any minute, Mom, puttering about upstairs, folding clothing, and pulling out pajamas, was going to call for them to brush their teeth. Mary would ask for ten more minutes, Mom would say no, Jude would start picking up the game, Mary would start arguing, complaining that Mom treated them like babies, while Dad, his feet in the air, reached for another pretzel.

But there was nothing normal about any of this.

"Well, I guess I'd better change," Father muttered, stepping to the tree and pulling an arm through the branches, needles burying themselves in his sweater. He rubbed his hands, disgusted, and, with a hand to his mouth, coughed. The phone rang. Jude didn't expect Father to answer it. Aside from the flurry of activity following the Freak Accident, Jude couldn't remember the last time Father was on the phone.

Another man, like a professional wrestler, had just jumped from a tree. If the vine snapped, he'd hit the forest floor with his face—that's what you were supposed to believe. Or not. Mother trotted from the laundry room and grabbed the phone. With a pop! like a struck match (Jude later wondered if he imagined this), the space behind the television wavered, like steam rising above a pot of boiling water, part of what would soon be Mary. On TV, the man hung a foot above the flat, blackened, earth. The women danced and their screams were as loud as the colors of their clothing.

Breathless, Mother answered the phone. "Hello?"

Jude waited for Father, still muttering, to leave the room. Registering the weight of a bad feeling—he didn't think Mary's appearance coinciding with the phone call was a coincidence—it was impossible to make out who Mother was speaking to.

Mary wasn't here to haunt anyone.

Yes, there was her secrecy, her screaming silence, but Jude drew on more evidence than this. Given her movements—that way, as if pushed, Mary left, or entered a room—Jude didn't think his sister could pass through objects. And while he wasn't sure, he doubted, if only because she had yet to do so, that she could touch, and consequently move, anything. Her presence was bizarre …

But Mary just wasn't spooky.

Initially, he had asked her dozens of questions, but she either couldn't, or was unwilling to answer them, so he stopped. Worse, given extended pauses between responses, or the way she couched certain phrases, it was obvious she experienced irritation, or, worse, that she became disappointed with him. Now, though? He couldn't help himself. It was clear that Mother was talking about him, and he needed to know what was happening. Finally, Father made for the foyer, and walked upstairs.

"Who is she talking to?" Jude said.

"How would I know?" Mary said. "Lower your voice."

"I don't know … I thought that, maybe, you know, you could be in two places at once, or something."

"How would that work?"

Jude shook his head. Exasperated, he regretted asking, the question sounding stupid as he was speaking. If she could materialize here, though, what would prevent her from … well from what, exactly?

She was right. Even if she could appear anywhere, she'd need to know where to go, first. But something was happening, Mother making it impossible to eavesdrop, her conversation consisting only of a series of "MmHms" and "I knows."

"MmHm," Mother said.

And then nothing. Just silence, as Mother listened to the person on the other end of the line, speaking.

And then, a couple moments later, "I know."

And then, "But tomorrow?"

And then nothing. Just more silence, as Mother did more listening.

"What is—" Jude said.

Mary raised a finger.

"MmHm," Mother said.

And then, a couple moments later, "I know."

"I really wish I knew who she was talking to," Jude muttered.

Mother poked her head into the living room. She said, "Yes?"

Mary shook her head.

Jude just looked at her.

Mother considered him for a moment, then, distracted by whomever was speaking, shook her head, and returned to the kitchen.

Mary shook her head. "You should be more concerned with who they are talking about."

What? Jude mouthed.

And then, from the kitchen, "Well, if you think so. MmHm."

And then, "James? Oh, I'm sure. There's nothing that he'd like more. It's not like we think Jude is taking advantage of the situation, but—"

"Taking advantage?" Jude whispered.

"It matters not, who she is talking to," Mary said. "Although I have a guess."

"Who?"

"It does not matter. But he thinks you should be back in school."

"Okay," Mother said. She was crying. Her voice caught. It was obvious that she was listening. And then she chuckled. And then she started laughing. "MmHm."

"He?" Jude hissed. "Back in school?"

"Yes, and thank you, Father," Mother said. She blew her nose. "Of course. Of course. We'll let you know how it goes. Yes. We're all in this together. Thank you."

"But she said that I didn't have to … she said …"

"Mother," Mary said, "is a liar."

"James?" Mother hung up the phone. She stepped into the living room. "Honey. Where's your father? I thought I heard—"

"He's changing."

"Changing?"

A Chinese man on the television licked a piece of paper, his blood forming a pretty impression, a bright red butterfly.

"Well, that's different," Mother said. Jude could not believe she didn't see Mary. She frowned. "There's nothing else on the television?"

Mary shook her head.

Jude remained silent.

"Well." Helen smiled. "Your father's changing, you said? Great. Hopefully he's getting to that tree. It really is becoming hazardous, don't you think?"

She made to leave the room, then, as if smacked on the behind, stood upright. "Can I get you anything? How about some ice cream?"

And Mary shook her head.

She stared as Mother walked from the room.

April 25, 1983

Nervous, Jude did not think the situation was going to get any better, but Mary, sitting beside him, insisted it would. Most of the vomit had hardened on his shirt, but, because he had a bloody nose, which continued to stream, his shirt was a slimy mess. The slime, which had oozed to pool on his lap, its consistency like an over-medium egg, slid as Father veered around Cascadilla Lake and accelerated up South Hill. Taking Triphammer Road to Endwell General, the goo not quite spilling off himself and onto the seat, but, rather, congealing to form a larger puddle, Jude coughed. Used tissues dotted the well beside his feet.

Rain fell heavily, drumming the roof of the car. Father's windshield wipers, whirring at their highest setting, cleared great sheets of water, and the sound and the motion added to Mother's panic and confusion.

"Don't tilt your head," Mary said. "Bleed."

Jude nodded, tucking his chin to his chest. He cupped his hands, catching dime-sized blood drops.

"Oh, honey, don't nod your head like that," Mother said, turning in her seat. "You don't want your nose to—" Exasperated, she dug through her purse. Why hadn't she taken a back seat?

Jude considered his mother. He opened his mouth to breathe, his teeth pink. Oxygen acted like an accelerant.

Bright red blood streamed over his top lip and into his mouth. He sputtered.

"Oh, Jude," Mother said. "Tip your head back, honey. And pinch your nose. It's the only way to stop that bleeding." She covered her mouth with a hand. "James, maybe you should pull over. I don't know what I was thinking, sitting up front like this."

"You're kidding," Father said, checking his mirrors. He cleared his throat.

"Puke," Mary said.

Jude was tired, he was unsure he had the energy.

"Do it," Mary said. And then, eying Mother, "Lean your head against the window, too."

Jude rested his forehead against the glass. It was cool. He knew he should listen to Mary. His sister was never wrong. Raindrops bulged from the window, or ran down the pane, long dizzy lines distorting his vision, pine trees and passing houses fluid shapes, their colors muted and blurred. The tires hummed, the vibration running the length of the car and shaking Jude's brain. He took a deep breath and held it, catching the air deep within his chest, as if working to make himself burp. He exhaled through his nose, expelling globs of snot and blood, and then quickly inhaled, swallowing as much of the gunk as possible.

Blech.

Gross.

Somehow, there was still some food in his stomach, and he lurched, coughing the mess into his hands.

"Good," Mary said.

Mother lowered her head. She wept.

Jude had been home from school for a couple of weeks, accompanying Mother when she left the house for the library, the SPCA, or Our Lady of the Lake. Helen, on their way to work, out of icebreakers, shared what she had learned from Mrs. Kruty, and, more importantly, facts she gleaned from Father Hours. While the altar, Mrs. Kruty would happily tell you, was 36" x 84" x 39" high, its mensa, a huge stone slate lifted from some nearby creek when the area was cleared to erect space for the cathedral, contained wondrous relics even she could not pretend to know, or understand.

Wasn't that interesting?

Jude nodded.

Since bringing Jude to work Mother had caught him talking to himself—what she called his imaginary friend. Jude offered resistance, but quieted when it became clear that his mother was in no mood for listening. While he was much too old to engage in such behavior, he had been through a lot. And she, an only child, had, for years, serious relationships with her dolls and stuffed animals, carefully naming each, and ascribing unto all unique personalities, holding elaborate sleepovers and parties. Part of her, she said, thought it healthy – a form of release. Her only concern was that, at times, he was incredibly serious, not so much talking, as listening.

The listening, his rapt attention, how it was that whomever (which is to say whatever) he engaged interested him more than his own parents—this was disturbing. She had yet to broach the subject with his father—he, too, had been through a lot, she pointed out, adding that he was terribly busy at work. If the behavior continued, or worsened, she was going to call Dr. Greene.

Her point?

The choice was Jude's.

And then, as if pretending the conversation had not taken place, she concluded by saying, "How about a real, grown-up, behind the scenes tour?"

Jude would have preferred the silence, solitude, and opportunity to spend time with Mary the nursery afforded, but Mother wasn't asking.

And so Jude nodded. He agreed.

Walking about the cathedral, Mother assumed many of those qualities in Mrs. Kruty Jude knew she despised. Speaking breathlessly, her bright eyes shining and pointed as punctuation marks, she underscored particularly salient points and interesting features.

"It's possible," she veered, making, as always, the conversation about herself. "It's really quite possible that everything that has happened is a sign. That God is calling us —and by "us" Jude knew she meant herself—for something far greater.

She never spoke of Mary's death, directly, and because there had not been time for her to believe she had done anything wrong—what had happened was so clearly unintentional that even the newspaper labeled the incident a Freak Accident—she underwent a strange mutation, her attitude a virulent variant, convinced that Mary's passing was a message, too. After all, God worked in mysterious ways.

Jude was not quite impressed—there was something about how much Mother knew about Our Lady of the Lake that was disturbing—but there was no doubting her acumen when, stopping by the altar, she fell into a familiar routine, one like Mrs. Kruty's constant proselytizing – as if an altar would ever play an important role in Jude's life, let alone interest him.

"Now the position of the altar," Mother said, "is not in any way random. There are guidelines that dictate where it should be placed. When a church is designed and built, the orientation of the church, along with the position of the altar, are planned out ahead of time to abide by set religious … by set Catholic standards.

"When a church is under construction, and it's being designed, the layout is such that the part people most like to see is always east. Which makes sense, of course, given that this is where the sun rises. So of course the altar, where we're standing, is east, and over there"—Mother pointed to the huge wooden doors—"that's west. Not that I expect you to remember this, but if these positions are reversed, with the altar on the west, and the entrance on the east? It's called occidentation."

Jude had listened because he was terrified of returning to school, but this did not change the fact that too many of her words were like wet matches: they stood for something, but were worthless.

"If a church cannot be built in a way to accommodate these positions, the terms 'east end', 'west door' and 'north aisle' are commonly used. The end that houses the altar is treated as the liturgical east, though it may not be the cardinal east. This has become more common in modern times with limited space in cities and strict building codes forcing changes to the way that churches are built and positioned.

"Point being," Mother said, leading them back to the nursery. Nothing is accidental. All of this ... everything you see has been carefully arranged. It's here, or there"—she laughed—"for a precise, set, purpose."

When alone, Jude explored the church, developing, in time, the nerve to enter those areas prohibited to all lay parishioners. But even Father Hours had made him promise to keep away from the tower. Contractors were working to preserve as much of the building as possible, while repairing significant structural damage. It was, Father Hours added, extremely dangerous. More so, presently, because they had run out of money, and had called off work for the foreseeable future.

"And I'm a priest," Father Hours smiled. "So you know I'm not lying."

Jude nodded.

"Trust me, Jude. I get it. Really, I do. Boy your age? Mysterious tower? I understand the appeal. It must seem terrific. But it's more than that. It's one of my favorite places on the planet. When I first started here, I would spend hours up there, reading, and writing. Now, not so much. I'm older. Fatter." He laughed, patted his belly. "Seriously, though. It really is dangerous. There are entire sections of floor so rotted that even a mouse would fall through. I'll take you up there one of these afternoons, though. At least to the top of the steps, the landing facing the west window. You can see all of Endwell. Well, practically, anyways. It truly is beautiful. You know what? Why wait. I'll speak with your mom, of course, but how about we check it out later this week? Be fun, don't you think? Break up the monotony."

Jude shrugged.

The priest had no way of knowing he had already visited the tower.

Jude had no desire to explore the tower, but Mary had been pushing the idea since Jude began skipping school and accompanying Mother to Our Lady of the Lake.

"It's easy for you to say," Jude had said.

Jude was sitting at a table in the nursery. The room's two doors were open, and he could see the altar, its coverlet removed. Adorned in hemp, more off-white than cream and interwoven with flaxen golden strands, the cere was the exact size of the mensa and, except for the added dimension the wax within the fabric afforded, was indiscernible. Purple side and front drops, steamed and pressed, were as crisp as their folds were precise. Mother had seen to this.

"I will tell you where to walk," Mary said. "There is no reason to worry."

"It's not that."

Mary waited.

"If I get caught, Mother will kill me."

"Kill you," Mary said.

Jude looked at Mary. Then laughed. "You know what I mean."

"You will not get caught," Mary said.

"But what if I do?" Jude stood and looked across the altar, towards the baptismal fountain. "It's so weird. I never have any idea where she is. What she's doing. When she's going to pop up. And you even told me yourself that you can't be in two places at once."

Mary waited.

"Plus, isn't the door locked?"

Jude immediately regretted asking. Either the key was accessible, and Mary, via Jude, had access, or the door wasn't locked. "Sorry."

"No reason to apologize. Just go to the top of the tower."

The nursery was silent. It wasn't much of a room. The carpeting was worn and thin, frayed, in spots, and lacked any definitive color. There were scuff marks on the walls. The space was not exactly dirty, but Jude would not call it clean. Yes, there was everything a mother needed for her child, and while everything was connected, nothing seemed affixed to anything. It was weird, and brought to mind his school's basement—which he had only heard about—and, because what he had heard was creepy, enjoyed drawing.

Like the nursery's closet.

Even though it was, this did not seem to be a part of the wall. Like something you could enter, but never escape. The pipes ran to and from the sink, but the feeling was that they didn't. Had there been an exposed light bulb and string dangling from the ceiling, this would not have looked out of place. This part of Our Lady of the Lake, which was supposed to be warm and inviting, was cold and disturbing, confusing in a way Jude couldn't put into words. It was like visiting a museum that didn't have any paintings. He didn't understand why Father Hours would spend years renovating the ceiling, a place no one would see, when the building needed work, down here.

"Why do you care? What's up there?"

"It is not about what is up there."

"What? I don't understand what the heck you're talking about."

"Like everything now, it is not what is, but how something seems."

"What does me climbing to the top of the tower seem like? And hey. If no one catches me, like you say? How can that seem like anything?"

"It is like I say. No one is going to catch you. You don't have to hide. You don't have to wear a mask or anything."

More than Mary flickering, or changing, the light in the room dimmed, and then brightened. Someone was coming.

As usual, it was Jude who would have to wait and see.

While Jude "felt warm," he didn't have a temperature, and possessed an appetite, eating heavy foods, like pizza, and meatball subs, getting sick not long after the fact. He didn't look ill. He didn't act ill. And, because Mother, for fear of making him ill, only fed him occasionally, he vomited less frequently. In this way she tricked herself into believing her boy was getting better.

The problem, Mother suggested, was that, while sick, his stomach had shrunk, and, now that he was getting better, she simply had to find agreeable foods. The answer, she offered Dr. Greene, was to feed him lighter fare. Dr. Greene agreed, and provided an array of dietary options.

He suggested that she keep a journal. If, in a week or two, the problem persisted? Well. They would cross that bridge. The plan, which she shared with Jude and Father before mass, was for Jude to eat gentle foods, like the white toast and apple juice she had placed before him, and return to school.

"The bus ride is probably a bit much," Mother said, sipping her coffee. "At least for now. So I'll just head to church early, drop you off, and, after work, pick you up, and drive you home. It's perfect."

To his right, bright as televised light, the sliding glass door shimmered like static. The sky, low and gray, obscured the tops of the trees, wisps of mist, what Jude considered almost-clouds, shrouding the house as if they lived at a much higher altitude. Rainfall had melted what remained of last week's surprise snowstorm, four or five inches of wet and heavy snow that, combined with the wind, took down branches and power lines. Positioned in front of the refrigerator, visible behind Mother's shoulder, Mary raised a finger. She shook her head. The directive was clear: Jude should not protest. At least not yet.

"Of course I'll be right downtown, too, so, if you don't feel well …" Mother set her cup on the table and folded her hands. "You know what? Why think negatively? Honey, listen. I'm sorry. I know you think we pushed you back too soon. And maybe we did. But we had a plan. Given that Winter and Spring Breaks were built into the calendar, we knew you could handle it. And, until you came down with this rotten bug, you were doing just fine. I"—she eyed Father—"well, your dad and I understand why you're nervous to return. Who wouldn't be? But I'm certain that if we just go slow and steady, act with an abundance of caution, you'll be right back to yourself by the end of the week. This is your new normal, honey. You'll feel like yourself in no time."

Cheered by her own pep talk, she stood from the table and cleared Father's plate. Rubbing his hands, Father coughed.

"Heck"—she set the dish in the sink—"after seeing all your friends? Getting some fresh air during recess?" She stood, hipshot against the counter, ankles crossed. "We'll have to celebrate," she said. "I can't remember the last time we went out to eat, just to, well, go out and eat. As a family."

Jude lifted his glass of apple juice and drank slowly, steadily. Most foods, if you vomited not long after eating, did not taste terrible. Chewing was also important. Chew well, and you puked baby food. If you hurried, because the food tasted great—or because you were really hungry— the sensation, if not the taste (or both), was like vomiting a big piece of celery, the effort both painful and blinding. Some foods, apple juice being one of them, tasted pretty much the same. Good even. Water was the worst. Water, on the way back up, tasted gross, like skin. Just the thought made him nauseous. The idea of returning to school, however, was terrifying. It was, in fact, much worse. Jude reached for another piece of toast. He chewed slowly and carefully. Once finished, he asked to be excused.

Mary followed Jude upstairs and into the bathroom— he always puked privately—and told him to wait.

"Why," Jude whispered. He ran the faucet, and, gross as it was, filled a paper cup with warm water. "I'm not going back. She thinks she can make me, but she can't." He swallowed the water and refilled the cup. "I can't tell you, Mary. I know how it sounds. Terrible. And it is terrible. But the feeling"—he gulped the water—"the feeling is so bad, so scary, not like I'm going to die, but something even worse." He wiped his mouth. "Like I'm going to do something terrible? I don't know what I feel. All's I know is that I'd rather be dead than go back to that place."

"She is Mother, Jude," Mary said. "She will do, and she will make you do, whatever she wants. Did you want to go back to school in January? Didn't she promise that you didn't have to go back until you were ready?"

They stood side by side, staring into the mirror. Hopeless, Jude reached forward to touch his sister's face. She remained in place, but his hand covered her reflection, skewing his perception, his fingers banging against the glass.

"Motherfuck." He lowered his hand. He wanted to lash out, but Mary wasn't the problem. She didn't deserve the words he had in mind. He studied the shower curtain. The pattern—black roses atop a bed of white roses—was confusing. The sight made him dizzy.

"You should have told me to tell those detectives about the bathtub," Jude said. "Back right after you died? I should have told them something. You don't think I know, but I know what she did. Her ways to punish you."

"I know that you know," Mary said. "It would be impossible for you not to know."

"Then why didn't you tell me to tell them?"

"Tell them what, Jude? That when I was five and refused to eat my broccoli Mother put me in the bathtub in my underwear? That she filled the tub with cold water until I did what she wanted?"

Jude nodded. Defiant, this was a fair question.

"Think about it, Jude," Mary said.

"Think about what?"

"Assuming they cared. And you are right, they would have. That is why they came to speak to Mother. To Father. But if there had been an investigation? What do you think would have happened to you? It is not like you would have been sent to live with Grandma."

"Grandma? What are you talking about? We haven't seen Grandma in ... I can't even remember the last time we've been to Long Island."

"That is the point. Imagine where you would be, right now, if there had been an investigation. She would never have been convicted, or found guilty, you know. You would be at home, living with her, and Father. Only all of Endwell would know. Mother would, in her "nice" way, make you the liar. Make you seem "bad." You hate school now? Imagine what living would be like if Mother suspected you had turned on her. Or if the kids from school heard from their parents the sort of parents you have. There is no winning. There is no winning that way."

He made to speak, and then stopped himself. He waited. Mary made sense. He, as if an actor, directed to read from a blank piece of paper, had no lines; had no idea what to say. His eyes burned and his throat hurt. If he wasn't careful, he was going to start crying.

"What happened. And what happens. These are not acts of hate." Mary faded. "She did not think she was doing anything wrong. Mother acted out of love. She is just a terrible lover."

"What? Love? How can you say that? No one hurts who you love."

She pointed to the running water. "Turn that off." And then, the air in the room still, "Mother is a fool. Mother is selfish. But Mother loves Father, and you, and she loved, and still does love, me. That, though, is the problem. Mother loves, but she does not know how to love equally. She is not balanced. She, more than you, needs medication.

"Of course you hurt the things you love. You hurt those you love more than just about anyone. You do not do so on purpose, you do not do so intentionally, but hurt, the ability to injure someone with our actions and our words, is what makes love possible. You cannot have coldness without warmth. You cannot be high if there is no low. Mother is not well, Jude. Who you, or, to be clear, who Mother is incapable of hurting, is the person she loves not at all."

"Stop it. You're confusing me."

"Mother is many things, but confusing is not one of them."

"Are you saying she hurts us on purpose? Why? Mother killed you, Mary! She didn't just hurt you, she went too far and she killed you."

Jude wept. With a loud cry and tears in his eyes Jude grabbed the sink. He didn't care that Mary was watching. All that her talking did was anger him. His body was sore and unforgiving. What arrived as sadness felt like relief. In this way he felt better. Stronger. "If you thought about someone other than Mother, you would know that you are hurting me."

"Mother hurts because she loves the wrong things too much. I do not expect you to understand … but one day you will."

Mother called from downstairs. In singsong, she said that it was time to go.

"Mother is calling you," Mary said.

The light in the room changed, the harsh fluorescence flashing, mellowing to become a brilliant amber.

Jude didn't want Mary to leave. He turned to face her, to—

"Do not worry," she said. "I know you want to, but do not puke. Not now. I am coming with you. Trust me, this will be better. Much better."

"What will?" Jude drew a forearm across his nose, took a deep breath.

Mary did not answer.

They left before Communion, the force of Jude's effort to vomit creating, as a bonus, a bloody nose. Puke both moist and stiff on his shirt, his nose crusted with blood, he seemed, to others, surprised, as if unsure what had happened. Father Hours raised the chalice and the host in the air, mumbling incoherently.

"Do not make it obvious, but push," Mary said. "This is good."

The church was full, and those parishioners sitting closest to the family had gathered their things, scattering as if Jude were on fire. Others slid down pews, creating space. Father Hours lowered the Eucharist, bowed, passed something off to Deacon Joe—a tall, Black man from Nigeria—and, head all but striking concrete, kissed the altar. A boy rang a bell. A vestige from a bygone era.

Mary stood before him, visible from the waist up, halved by the back of a pew. Jude cocked his head, unsure.

"Like you are blowing your nose. No. Like you are trying to make your face red. Yes. Like that. Do not look, but you should see Mother."

"Oh, Helen," Mrs. Kruty whispered, waddling down their pew. In her blacks and blues she looked like a plum. "And Jude, you poor thing!" She reached out a hand, then slowly retracted. "My goodness," she whispered, more quietly. "He's bleeding. Should he—"

"Thank you, Mrs. Kruty," Helen smiled. "He's just been fighting a little bug." Helen spoke loudly, as if her response might calm those still scattering. The Bendzes were well-known.

"Oh, but his face. And it being so warm in here."

Jude laughed. Mother and Mrs. Kruty frowned.

"Jude," Mary warned. "Pretend you are coughing."

He didn't know what was funny, but there was something about Mother and Mrs. Kruty, how they considered the condition of candleholders and the constitution of a sick and bleeding child with the same degree of concern, that struck him as absurd. Nodding, he affected to gag, and then began coughing, spraying blood all over his hands.

It was warm. Father Hours had not ordered maintenance to run the air conditioning. Normally, the large doors fronting the church would be open, allowing for a cool breeze. But it was pouring, and the wind and the rain, which picked up during the homily, had yet to relent, and was overwhelming, drowning out all other sound, and so the doors had been closed, the wooden pews sticky with humidity.

Because it was so warm, Father was wearing a light sweater in lieu of a jacket. He removed the sweater and made to clean the mess, but Mrs. Kruty stood, waved a hand.

"Go, go, go, go, go!" she said. "I'll get a custodian."

Mother gritted her teeth and stared at Father. He cleared his throat and held his sweater in both hands, uncertainly.

"Father is so hopeless," Mary said.

"We're just going to clean this and—"

"I won't hear of that," Mrs. Kruty said. She didn't move any closer, but she made it clear she wasn't leaving. "You just get your little Jude on home, or to the ER, and I'll find one of the custodians directly."

"Or to the ER," Mother mumbled, rising, ripping Father's sweater from his hands and mopping the vomit from the pew, working with her back to Mrs. Kruty until the woman, flustered, disappeared.

"Appearances," Mary said.

"What?" Jude said.

"What?" Mother looked over her shoulder.

"Huh?" Jude said, a hand to his face, blood dripping from his fingers to the floor. "I didn't say anything."

Helen wasn't exactly a liar. She, were you to ask, simply provided her account of the truth. Given enough time, though? Helen could lie, and convincingly.

What's more (they were speaking to an intake nurse at Endwell General), James would not contradict her. To the degree he knew anything, what happened at home was Helen's business. She could no more hold court with a cohort of IBM executives concerning a delay in a component of the B-2 Spirit's defense system, than he could scramble an egg. Facing a direct line of questioning, however, when the first lie meant fabricating another, Helen faltered, fear of discovery, more so than moral uncertainty, pinning her in place. Helen was smart. She knew that truth had teeth.

Regardless, Jude was admitted.

Quickly, Jude regretted listening to Mary.

The beds on the floor were reserved for old men and older women with dry coughs and heart conditions. These were people who didn't lie down, exactly. It being too painful to rest. It being too painful to move. Elbows on mattresses enabled hands to support great heads of disheveled hair. Or forearms covering closed eyes. Efforts, these, to erase the too bright light. Like drunks, they peered at everything with one eye closed.

Like Mary, these were people who didn't quite speak … at least, so far as Jude could tell, to others. Like Mary, they could point. Like Mary, they could nod. And so hanging on the walls were posters of emojis, a visual language, animated approximations of pain set in ranges of ten, simple smiley faces black and white, their expressions ranging from one (placid) to ten (eyes x's of pain, sweat, or tears, all but bursting off the page).

His lone neighbor sat upright in bed, stock-still, buried beneath a mound of bright white blankets. Her bad hand positioned on a stack of pillows, the other clutched the top of her gown. Gasping, bug-eyes bright, the woman appeared to be staring into some bizarre, frightful dimension, and was horrified by what she saw.

Attending nurses looked irritated, or, worse, bored. As if they'd rather be someplace else. They spoke too loudly, drawing out their vowels as if speaking to young children. The women didn't hide their irritation, which edged upon hostility, understanding that they, one way or another, would not see these individuals much longer. When opening and closing the blue cloth curtains which hung from arced tracks in the ceiling, they muttered to no one in particular. Sitting, when able, they released great sighs from their positions at the nurses' station, sipping Coke through straws rising from their bright red cans, and crunching potato chips while staring at computer screens.

Cleaned up and administered an IV, Jude, warm beneath the covers and comfortable in a thin, cotton, medical gown, watched WWF on the wall-mounted TV. He refused both a juice box and a ginger ale. A nurse placed these drinks atop his bedside table. Mother and Father were missing.

"I can't believe Mother agreed to pay for TV," Jude whispered.

Mary stood in front of a curtain, a white cutout stark against the pale blue fabric. This made her blue eyes brighter, her dark brown hair in sharp contrast within the room's unrelenting fluorescence. The blips and the beeps from the area's machines were rhythmic and soothing, and Jude relaxed.

"It is about appearances," Mary said. "Mother knows she looks bad."

"Huh? I don't know what you mean."

"Not taking you to see a doctor, a real doctor, sooner. Dr. Greene is for head colds and sore throats. Plus, she has lied to him. Many times. She wants to look like she cares."

"Oh," Jude said.

He was tired. Being sick when you were well wasn't easy. And the way Mary spoke was confusing. Since there was nothing he could do, it was nice, for once, not to be called upon to do anything. He relaxed. For the first time since

Mary died, he was not afraid. He was not terrified of hurting someone. Or something. But Mary cared, and he didn't want her to leave. He said, "Now what are they doing?"

"You are being admitted. This requires paperwork and a lot of time."

"Admitted? I don't get it."

Mary explained, though he wasn't paying much attention. Mother didn't let him watch wrestling, and a man in shiny blue spandex was climbing the side of the ring. Jude smiled, amazed, when the man jumped from the top rope and kicked his opponent—a hairy, fat man wearing a black leotard—in the face, bounced up from the ring, and started stomping around in a circle.

"So they really think I'm sick? They're doctors, Mary, how can they get that wrong?"

"They do not know anything other than what Mother and Father tell them, and how you present yourself to them."

"Present?"

"A fancy word for looking. As in how you appear to them, medically." She faded. "Obviously, if you do not eat you will die. They have no reason to believe you are not sick. Mother was so nervous she did not even tell them about me. About what happened. They called Dr. Greene and he must have said something, because they asked Mother and she started crying. I did not die that long ago. They are not making a connection with what is going on with you, and what happened with me. Necessarily. Obviously this is something they have thought about. Considered. But I am pretty sure they have ruled this out. It matters very little, what they think. What we must do is to get what they consider to work in your favor. But let me worry about that. You have been convincing. You have done a good job, brother. You have them thinking. But they told Mother and Father you need to stay here, for tests. And observation."

The wrestler in the leotard raked his opponent's eyes and kicked him in the groin. The referee pushed him back into a corner, and the two began arguing. The wrestler punched the referee, knocking him unconscious. Recovered, the wrestler in blue slid off the canvas mat, grabbed something from a table near a row of fans, and returned; he was carrying a 2 x 4, which, true to form, he wielded like a baseball bat. His opponent, seeing the weapon, raised his hands in fear and shook his head. He fell to his knees, begging for mercy.

"All they know, because Mother lied, is that you have been vomiting, 'on and off,' for the past couple of weeks. And, well, that you have had a bloody nose. That is evident. Mother told them you love school. She told them that before, the first time you refused to go to school, but she made you? Well, she left that part out. She told the doctors you were cleared by the psychiatrist, and that the psychiatrist did not find anything wrong with you."

"But I didn't say anything to that woman, how could she say I was okay?"

Mary did not reply.

"So I'm going to stay here?"

"Not here," Mary said. "This is the Emergency Room. You are going to a different part of the hospital. Because you are a child you will get your own room. Or you may have a roommate your own age. They are going to run tests. Because you are right, the doctors do have it all wrong, they think you may have a parasite."

"Huh? What's that?"

"Worms. Or something like that."

"That's gross."

Mary faded. Jude was content to sit in silence. His chest burned, and talking hurt. It was worth it. School was horrible, but home wasn't much better. Here, though. This was nice. There was no pressure. It had only been a few hours, and while things happened, things happened around him. Like Mary, in a way, all he had to do was be. Like Mary, he was kind of dead. As usual, she was right. Puking at church was better than puking at home. He liked it here, and he wanted to stay.

The man in blue smashed the board across the other man's face, knocking him flat on his back. The wrestler tossed the weapon out of the ring and the crowd cheered. The camera showed the referee, who, sitting with his legs splayed, realized the man in blue was pinning his opponent. Like a snake the referee slid in on his belly and, with a hand, slammed the mat once, twice …

"You should have seen Mother's face when they went over your condition," Mary said.

The fat wrestler wiggled and wobbled his way until he was sitting, his thick white legs bright and hairy. The man in blue, shocked, stood up, and, shouting, shoved the referee. The fat man got to a knee, and then pushed himself upright, making to kick his opponent in the back, but he was too slow. The wrestler in blue turned and caught his foot. The other man affected fear and started praying, saying he was sorry. The man stood there, holding his foot, eyes bright, looking around at the crowd, wildly. The people screamed and cheered.

"Appearances," Jude said, watching the match end, and cut to commercial.

There wasn't much in the room. The nurse, after applying the IV (his vitals were poor, and he was dehydrated), moved the table out of reach. The TV's remote was on the table. Jude sighed. He was too nervous to pull on its cord, fearing the giant device would fall and hit the floor.

"Sometimes I wish you could, like—"

"It is bad enough, what she did to me," Mary said. "Could you imagine if she had two dead kids? If both of her twins died before middle school? Even though they did not catch her, and never will, the looks people would give her, the thoughts they would have about her. Forever."

Mary faded. If Jude didn't know better, he would have sworn she had smiled.

Jude didn't hate Mother as much as Mary. He didn't like her that much, either, but didn't Mary just say that she loved him, and her, as well? Mary wasn't lying, but maybe Mother wasn't lying, either. That's what made a Freak Accident a Freak Accident, right? And the police, the detectives, they wouldn't give up so easily, would they?

Behind Mary and beyond the curtain the nurses at their stations, dressed in scrubs, waited for the day's disasters to come wheeling their way. These women were nothing like Mother. Maybe Mother was the disaster. Maybe Mother was the person who knocked people off their feet, leaving them to be picked up, pushed about on wheels. Jude didn't know. And Jude was getting tired of caring.

"I am sorry, Jude," Mary said. "But Mother, until she is punished. Well. She can never be forgiven …" She drifted. "Do you know what bulimia is? Anorexia?"

Jude didn't.

"It is when you purposefully do something to make yourself skinny. Or to get attention."

"But I don't want attention." He lifted an arm. Was transfixed by the IV. "And look. I'm already skinny."

"I know, Jude. And, right now, no one has any reason to think you want attention, or that you are worried about your weight."

"That's good," Jude said. "Isn't it?"

"Yes," Mary said. "The doctors are not concerned. But …" She drifted, the sounds of the ER swelling around them. "Technically, you are killing yourself. But I knew this would never work."

"What would never work? Killing myself? What're you talking about? You're confusing me, again. Actually, you're freaking me out. Things are going great. You said so, yourself. Let's just let them do whatever. At least for a while. I'm tired, Mary. You do remember what that is, don't you? How people actually get tired?"

Mary ignored him. "The good news is that bulimia and anorexia is pretty much a girl thing. Yes. You have suffered a tragedy. But again. The doctors, like everyone, believe Mother. That should tell you something. And not about the doctors. How this goes from here is up to you. How well you make yourself puke. At least for a while. If they catch on, and they will, then we—"

Mother appeared on the other side of the curtain. She had asked a question and was listening. A doctor, tall and thin, with a thick black beard and a shock of dark black hair, drew back the curtain and entered the room. Mother and Father followed. He introduced himself as Dr. Kush and asked Jude how he was feeling. He slid a stethoscope beneath Jude's gown, and, listening to Jude's heart, frowned. Satisfied, he straightened, placed the stethoscope on Jude's back, and listened to him breathe. Nodding, he straightened, and told him a watered-down version of what was happening. He asked if Jude had any questions.

Mary nodded.

"Yes," Jude said.

The adults looked at Jude and waited. After a few moments Dr. Kush said, "Yes? Go on."

Mary raised a finger across her lips.

"Well then," the doctor said, impatiently. "In the—"

"I'm sure he's just overwhelmed," Mother said. She stepped to Jude's side, placed a hand on his forearm. "Did you have a question, honey? Go on. Ask Dr. Crust. It's okay."

Irritated, the doctor checked his pager. "Kush"—he shook his head—"it's Doctor …" He shrugged off the thought, frowned. "I'm afraid I have to go. But time is on our side. I'm glad you have questions, Jude. It's important that you take control of your health. Right now, let's get one of the nurses to dim these lights, and you can have a nap. I'm sure you could all use a good rest. It'll be a bit before we have a bed," he addressed Mother and Father. "But you're in good hands." He looked as if he were about to say something, and then, as if thinking better of it, left the room.

Father paced about the room before stopping at the foot of Jude's bed. He coughed, as if something were caught in his throat. "I'm going to stretch my legs. Can I get anyone, anything?"

Mother frowned, found the remote, took the room's only chair, and repeatedly flipped through the channels before, with a sigh, settling on The Home Shopping Network.

"Hot tea," she said.

But it was too late. James had already disappeared behind the curtain.

DECEMBER 25, 1982

Although Mary didn't speak for over an hour, she had, directly following her first apparition, raised a finger to her lips, ordering Jude silent, a gesture she had made one million times before, when, alive and up to no good, she heard their mom coming. Jude knew Mary was real, and that there was no reason to be scared, either. His sister would never hurt him, and even though she remained silent, and, somewhat creepily, stood behind the TV blankly staring, at times difficult to distinguish, as if eaten by the television's glare, she was here to help, there could be no other reason. Of this, Jude was certain. For the first time since the Freak Accident, Jude was motivated to move, and he wanted to do something other than sit. Only Mary, reading his mind, violently shook her head. He nodded.

"Hmmmm?" Mother said. She was sitting on the other end of the sofa, feet flush with the floor, hands on her knees.

"I didn't say anything," Jude said.

"Oh."

Mary nodded. She lowered her finger.

Two hours earlier, driving across Endwell's West Hill. The moon a scythe high atop the fallen sky, its light slashing through wide swathes of darkness to make Alice Blue the snow-covered hillsides, what remained of Jude's family drove home. Alien landscape, this lonesome country road. Overhead, stars glittered like snowflakes. Around them, snowflakes fell, illuminated by Father's headlights, glittering bright as stars. They passed trailers outlined in huge strings of color. They passed old farmhouses, electric candles filling windows with white. In that front yard a snowman. Over there? Kids in puffy snowsuits running, sledding, and making angels from the snow. Like something ripped from a movie, this time of year.

Father pulled into their heated garage and killed the engine. No one moved. Ice and slush melted to drip and plop from wheel wells. No one moved. Mother's expression was a combination of anger and anguish Jude didn't understand. All he wanted to do was sit. It was hard to imagine doing anything other than sitting. The temperature inside the car cooled, then dipped to become uncomfortable.

"Let's go," Father said, opening his door. He cleared his throat.

The smell of concrete and gasoline and fallen snow and old newspapers mixed to become one thing: a memory. "Come on, Helle. Jude."

Jude stared through the windshield. He was not ready to move. The garage was very dark. Shapes once black and indiscernible, nebulous masses dripping from pegboards, strange floating globs, Jude watched them shimmer slowly as they swirled, as they gained form and dimension from their places upon wooden shelving and with this added dimension shapes became objects, and these objects assumed meaning—like words—both real and inconsequential. Jude was not interested in any of it. But he was conscious of how he looked—and how he must look. Closing his eyes, he pushed pictures of Mary being dead from his mind and did his best to imagine nothing, instead.

Only nothing, apparently, was not an option. Like a commercial, images of Mary crashed in upon his consciousness, and though he looked around the garage and thought the words pegboard, shelf, hammer, and nail, all he saw was his sister, blue, and growing bluer on the kitchen floor. It was cold. He shook his head. He worked to erase the sight from his mind. Father opened his door and gently pulled Jude by an arm, a shoulder. Jude did not mind being led.

They kicked off their boots before entering the kitchen and slid into their slippers, silent, no one speaking. They passed through the kitchen. The deck was illuminated—someone forgot to kill the light—and the trampled snow where Mother and Father had found Mary and carried her into the kitchen created weird shadows. There were towels on the floor. It was snowing, but softly, the sort that amounted to nothing, that, otherwise, would have been pretty. Noise drifted from the television, and Jude entered the living room. Mother followed and joined him on the sofa, taking the opposite end. Erect, she sat without moving, her feet flush with the floor, her hands on her knees.

Father crossed the room and crouched, reaching behind presents and pulling from a socket the cord illuminating their Christmas tree. The huge Douglas fir loomed in the corner to Jude's right, near the picture window, that place where their cove ceiling reached its greatest height. Just like that, the room was much darker, moonlight making distinct blue points on many of the ornaments. The shattered family's pile of presents, carefully arranged beneath the tree's bottom boughs, remained unopened because their tradition was presents after mass, and this only if Mary and Jude had behaved.

Mother would later donate the gifts to Our Lady of the Lake.

But presently …

Administered a shot and sent home with a bottle of medication, Mother was a puddle, a series of involuntary actions. Dressed for mass in black slacks and a black knit sweater, mascara had clumped in ragged clusters around her eyes. Her face was gray, and her makeup made outlines of her tears. Red with lipstick, her mouth slackened, as if sliding off her face. She looked like a terrible clown. She wore a pin—a green wreath, a Christmas present from Father—and matching earrings. She was a balloon, slowly losing air. Jude did not like looking at her.

Father placed a hand on Jude's shoulder. Opening his mouth as if to speak, he lowered his head. He dropped his arm. He coughed, as if something was in his throat.

So. It was even stranger between them.

Father left the room. From the kitchen the sound of the tap running, of a glass set on the counter, of the refrigerator opening. He brought Mother a glass of water, a can of Coke, and two tiny green pills. Mother swallowed these mechanically, with a gulp of water. Father watched. He took the glass and set the water and the can of Coke on an end table.

"I should make a few calls."

"Ah," Mother said.

Father cleared his throat. He left the room.

The television spit shadows as scene cut to scene, or the program jumped to a commercial, and Mary, with the pop! of a blown fuse, emerged. Materialized. As if needing new batteries she flickered and faded, before, in time, growing brighter, becoming what Jude would later consider fully luminous. A finger before her lips she stood, impassionate, interrupted only by the TV's bright light, unbelievably still, completely motionless.

Stunned, Jude, as if falling from some great height, passed directly through anything like sentimentality—that, and other emotions, would arrive later—to become anxious. Overwhelmed. It was not easy, breathing.

He did not doubt that before him, standing there behind the TV, was his sister. Was Mary. But, as he considered what he saw—heart thudding, back sweating—parts of himself, elements of awareness he never before knew he possessed, created discomfort.

The problem with reading so many books, and with watching so many movies, was that reality, presented as such, is so misaligned, and on such a warped scale, that people, in time, intuitively grasp those essential principles aligned with existence slightly incorrectly. There is no truth. If anything, the opposite holds true. Of truth, Jude thought nothing. It was only because Jude was shocked, that because Jude believed what he saw before him was real, that he was able to do what Mary demanded ... which, at least presently, was absolutely nothing.

Mother rose from the sofa, toed off her slippers and socks, and lifted her glass of water from the end table. She sat back down, ankles crossed, and returned the water, clasping her hands on her lap.

Mother did not believe in ghosts. She was also on drugs. Maybe this was why she didn't see Mary? Either way, Jude almost smiled. Mary was right there! Standing right there in front of them! Almost as much as seeing Mary, it was the secrecy that made him happy. Mary was real. As real as a ghost could be, anyways. Jude played it cool. Mary nodded.

After a while, when he couldn't take it any longer, he said, "You can go, you know," he said.

"Hmmmm?" Mother said.

"If you wanted to lie down, or something? I'll be okay."

"Oh. Why honey. Dear. That's so kind of you. I'm fine, though. But thank you. I'll be fine right here."

Jude looked to his sister. Mary remained motionless, a finger to her lips.

And then, moments later …

"Jude," Mother said. She shuddered, bent forward, grabbing her footwear. "I think I need to lie down. But I will be awake, if you need anything. Do you need anything? You don't need anything, do you?"

Jude shook his head. For fear of giving away his secret, he didn't want to look at Mary. But he couldn't stand to look at his mother, either. It was obvious that she didn't know what she was talking about. That she wanted to be alone. He looked at her glass of water.

"I see you're looking at my glass of water."

"What?" Jude said.

"You're looking at my water glass. I thought you might like a glass of water?"

"No."

"Ah," Helen said. She stood and made for the foyer.

Relieved, Jude settled into the sofa, and he waited for Mary to give him a sign. Mother called his name. Jude looked at Mary. She nodded. Jude got up and met his mother at the foot of the stairs. She was staring at a pair of Mary's sneakers and winter boots, piled in a corner.

"Have you seen your father?" Mother had a foot on the first step, and she held her socks and slippers in one hand, the glass of water with the other. She had left her Coke on the end table.

"Why?" Jude said. "Do you need him?"

"I'm afraid"—Helen looked up—"I'm not sure I can do this."

Much cooler than the living room, the foyer smelled clean, and crisp, like wind and snow. The seal surrounding the front door needed repair, and cold air emanated from the wood. Father must be in his office. Jude stepped around his mother and took the stairs. He would tell Father that Mother was, what? Stuck?

Halfway up the stairs, Father called out from the kitchen. Jude stopped, confused. His father had not been upstairs after all. Strange.

"Helen?" Father coughed and cleared his throat.

Jude turned as Father stepped into the foyer. And for a moment it was like that. Jude looking at Father, and Father looking at Mother, and Mother looking at Jude, as if he were leading the way.

Father's pants were wet. From his thighs to his waist the khaki was a heavy, shadowy tan, colored with moisture, and he stood with a confused, pained expression. He had not expected to find his family. He swallowed, with what appeared to be difficulty.

Conscious more of love than fear, Jude, from the beginning, directed his eyes not towards the dead, finding within Mary's first apparition nothing supernatural, and nothing by way of reunion. Here was an offering, a sense of reconciliation. Like his parents and their God, Jude did not feel compelled to concern himself with what he didn't know. With what seemed impossible. He would place his faith in Mary. He did not feel better, but comforted … no longer, he realized, so very afraid.

Jude made for the television, to change the channel, but Mary shook her head, she told him to sit on the sofa. In sound, her voice was the same.

"How do—"

Mary raised a finger to her lips. "Quiet. You are too old to talk to yourself. To have an imaginary friend. It is not natural. If Mother or Father hear you talking they will think you are talking to me, and that you are not well. Do you understand?"

Jude opened his mouth, he was going to say 'yes,' but Mary shook her head.

"You can read my mind?" he whispered.

"I could always read your mind," she said. "At least when we were twinning. Well, at least in a way. But yes. Now, even more so than before, I feel what you are thinking. It is not exactly what you, or people like Mother think of as a thought, or thinking, but yes. I feel what you want to say. This is because I understand how you feel. Words. Those are just extra things. People invented the wrong way of communicating. One day you will see. Perhaps one day soon."

Confused, Jude could not stop himself speaking. This was way too weird.

"How come you can talk normally?" Jude whispered, jumping topics. "Well, you sound sort of weird, but you know what I mean."

"We can never be stilled, but we are, often, silenced. Mother and Father cannot see or hear me, and I am unsure how much time I have, with you, here. Reason, and by this I mean how Mother and Father, and you, think, knows absolutely nothing. Not that it matters. Even in death Mother would have me dead, rather than permit my presence to dilute her fascination with faith. Or interrupt her time, sitting on the sofa, in front of the Home Shopping Network."

"You sound so much smarter. Like Dad."

"Father?" Mary pointed upstairs. "He is smart. But he, also, is not smart. Now, I am neither, as well." She lowered her hand.

Confused, Jude circled back. "You think Mom wanted to kill you, or do you mean God and Jesus and stuff? I don't understand. You're confusing me."

She nodded.

Whatever. Jude cracked Mother's Coke—an action, ordinarily, he wouldn't dream of doing—and took a sip. "Have you seen God?"

There was a long pause, what Jude would soon come to think of as Mary fading. Having no idea what was happening, he waited. Mary certainly looked dead. Nothing about her echoed humanity. Her hair—long and curly, and, most importantly, dry—and eyes—fierce as fire—belied what happened that morning, and how she appeared on the kitchen floor before the ambulance arrived, shaking, convulsing, Mother shrieking, Father standing with a hand over his mouth …

But, when considering her now, and trying to assemble what she was, being dead, he was unable to find the right words. While her voice was the same, the way she spoke was different, her cadence slow, stilted, and deliberate. He followed her in the moment, and understood the individual words coming from her mouth, but she spoke like a grownup, and her tone so put him at ease that he had trouble remembering what she said. He was lost. She had lost him. He heard the men on the TV, talking. Mary didn't glow, not exactly, but, like the TV, she was both physical, and made of light … or so she seemed.

"It is not a secret," Mary said. "It is more that people do not know."

"Don't know what?" Jude whispered.

"That there are other ways to be. Worse, people do not believe the few people who do know. Those people who, like you, can see. They, the others, pray to God. And that is okay. But you, and people like you, they call ghouls."

"You sound like these old guys on TV."

Mary did not respond.

"Can you only come out at night?"

"No. But set your mind on what I tell you, not what you see."

"Sure," Jude whispered. "Okay. But if I was dead, and you were talking to me? To my ghost? You'd have questions too, Mary. You would, you know."

"Ghost," Mary said.

"Yeah, ghost," Jude said. "That's what you are, right?"

Sweat broke out across his body, and he felt nauseous. Disoriented and uncertain. A little bit dizzy. He could not feel the sofa, and, for a quick, fleeting moment, believed that he was falling. He flattened his hands against the cushions and steadied himself. It was difficult to think.

Mary did not blink. She did not move. White, but not quite bright, there was nothing warm or comforting about her, other than that she wasn't gone, that she was here, with him. In that moment he realized how much he loved her … how much he had always loved her. But while he wanted to touch her, to reach out and hug her, all she wanted was for him to whisper.

Jude's throat tightened, and he had trouble swallowing. His eyes filled with tears. "I never thought I'd see you again."

"Of course not. That is how you have been conditioned. You are not listening, Jude. No one else can hear, or see me, because no one else believes that their minds are closed."

Jude went to tell her that she wasn't making sense, but changed his mind. It must be weird being a baby ghost.

"I cannot witness everything, but I do see things you cannot see or hear."

"So Mom is right about God?"

"Do you see God?"

Jude admitted that he didn't.

"I am not here to reveal secrets, but to expose the truth. For this to work, though, if you want us to be together again, I need you to be strong, you cannot be weak, and you cannot be afraid."

Mary faded. A wind gust flattened against the side of the house. The world stilled, and then rose again. A shelf of snow slid from the roof, thudding below the picture window. Absently, Jude wondered if Mary knew where the wind came from. He wondered if, in being dead, she now knew why.

Mary was wrong. Just because he was often wondering—who wouldn't be?—he was listening. She was just too confusing. Jude tried to tell her this, but she either didn't hear him, couldn't hear him, or chose not to respond. He did not feel brave because there was no reason to be afraid. But this wasn't the same thing as saying he wasn't scared. He smiled. Some of what Mary said—or how she said what she meant—was making sense.

Mary's presence, strange as it was, was comforting. This was all that mattered. He wanted to be with her. To that end, he would do what she said. The television program blinked off and on to a commercial.

It was eleven o'clock. Time for another show.

APRIL 12, 1983

His footfalls startled a charm of finches, and, for a moment, Jude forgot his fear of heights, amazed how the birds fell from atop the tower to streak across the sky in one great pattern seemingly preordained, as if possessed by some unified and perfect symmetry. Like studied patterns of falling snow, these birds. As if caught by a great wind gust they rose and swiftly fell, veered and smoothly careened. And it was in identifying, and then following the flight of an individual bird; it was in watching the animal gather speed, how the bending angle of sunlight upon a single wing lent dimension, afforded to one bird—and this one of what, one hundred? one thousand?—a definitive shape (only a shape unlike that of any artist's rendering; an image unlike anything Jude had ever seen); before, in the near-distance, the birds blended to inform a dark mass low above the horizon and, as one, fell from the sky, alighting upon a field adjacent Cascadilla Park.

Storm clouds had built over the water, and the lake was unsettled, a blur more white than blue. Losing sight of the birds, Jude caught his reflection in the glass of the tower's west facing window. Hard to believe he was still inside Our Lady of the Lake. Leaning against the wall, he fought a wave of dizziness.

Mary stood behind Jude, halved by the stairwell's sheer angle, as, when dipped into dark water, you lose sight of a hand and wrist at the forearm. Luminous within the uniform of relative darkness, her blue eyes bright, her dark hair framed her thin, pale face. Mary wanted him to move, but Jude was frightened. He never should have let her talk him into this.

"You are afraid of heights."

Jude raised a hand as if to say: And?

"Yet you just walked all those steps."

Jude didn't want to think about the steps.

Mary never understood why her brother was afraid of heights, but she never had any real reason to find out. To directly ask.

Jude shrugged. "I don't know. Why were you ever scared of anything?"

"I was not scared of anything."

"That's not true," Jude said, looking around the space. "What about spiders? And needles, as well?"

The tower was dark, cool, and quiet. Where Jude expected cobwebs, or dust, there was only exposed wood. If the space was under renovation, there was no evidence of this.

"I hated spiders. Needles resulted in pain. That is what you would call causality. But I was not scared of either. I avoided both. There is a difference."

"Well, I avoid heights."

"Look up."

Jude shook his head.

"Jude," Mary said. "Trust me. The reason you are afraid of heights? It is all in your mind. I am not saying that what you are feeling is not real, but the danger is not real. What your body is telling you is a lie. Mother has been up here dozens of times, and she has never suffered so much as a splinter."

"Yeah, well, I'm not Mother."

Mary moved her hands above the railings.

"What is happening is natural. Your body is reacting. But your mind can overcome what is bothering you. There is something I would like to show you. There is a space I think you will like. But I need you to move. I must get past so that I can show you. You"—Mary made to move—"you are afraid of the wrong thing. What you need to worry about is the floor. If anything."

Jude pressed a hand against the wall, closed his eyes, and then, with the back of his head against the wood, looked up. His legs buckled, but he straightened. He took a deep breath. Above him light dissipated into shadow, and, ultimately, darkness. He calmed, but it took a moment.

"See?" Mary said, rising, and, in that way of hers, moving, as if pushed, around the remaining steps, sliding past her brother, nearly brushing his body. She faced the window.

"Life is a balancing act. From where you are standing right now?" She eyed Jude, and then the steps spiraling to the ground floor. "You couldn't hurt yourself if you tried. Well, that is not entirely true." She mimicked rapping the pole running from floor to ceiling, that which secured each step and spindle. "You could give yourself a nice bump on the head, or bust a lip, but that is about it."

Jude grabbed the railing and looked down. Mary was right. He would only make it four or so steps before a curve in the construction stopped his progress. More importantly—there was not enough space between the stairwell and the walls for him to fit. It was impossible for him to fall. Unless the building collapsed, he was, at least while standing here, safe.

A wind gust flattened against the side of the tower. Moments later, raindrops spit against the glass. A dormant fly buzzed to life. The insect worked its way to the top of the window's screen, rising to the wooden frame and then falling, as if jolted by electricity, landing with a plunk on the splintered pane. From the other end of the building church bells called out a quarter hour.

"Have you—" Jude stopped. "How many times have you been up here?"

Mary moved from the window to occupy a narrow corridor. The space was black, totally without light. As ghost, his sister had never appeared so pretty, so bright. Like a piece of white paper, she was complete, and total, illuminating nothing, an apex presenting, simply, the essence of herself.

"What is the matter?" she said.

"Nothing." Jude's throat tightened, and his eyes filled with water.

"You are lying," Mary said.

The fly rose and loped about the stairwell. Buzzing mechanically, it returned, bouncing, repeatedly, against the screen. Tired, it clung to the wire, walking its way to the top. Was the fly here, in this space above Jude, during Mary's funeral? Did the insect make its way inside before the doors closed and the ceremony silenced the congregation? Strange. Jude didn't often think of that service.

Jude shook his head. "It's just so weird, sometimes. You being here, but not being here?" He wiped an eye with the palm of a hand. "And you would like this more than anyone. Seeing you?" He wiped his nose with the back of an arm. "You know what I mean. Being able to see a ghost. And what good is it anyways, seeing a ghost, if you can't tell anyone?"

"There are many things I do not know. Knowing how I would feel if I were you is one of them."

Jude raised his head and closed his eyes. He made fists of his hands. Rain lashed the window. The storm worked to make the space inside the tower feel compressed, completely still. He looked at his sister. Bright eyes wide open, Mary almost looked asleep.

More than anything, she seemed haunted. And not necessarily that she was the ghost, but that she was the one sought after. Targeted. No. That wasn't right. It wasn't that Mary seemed so much targeted as … alarmed. Uneasy. Jude avoided her eyes. They made him think of her being dead. Could someone, or some thing, be after Mary? While possible, Jude didn't think so. Of course he couldn't possibly know, but he didn't see how. Mary had never done anything wrong. What, then? All that Jude could think of was himself. That she was bothered by him.

After all these months, Jude didn't understand what she was able to see. How his sister's eyes didn't shine or reflect anything. How it wasn't like she looked at anything but, rather, that her eyes were signs. Such deep pockets of mystery. He understood Mary wanted him to follow, that she intended to lead him down the corridor, but he didn't want to go.

"You have a flashlight," Mary said. "Do not worry, I will tell you where to set your feet."

It was true. Jude had taken a flashlight from a drawer in the nursery before following Mary down the hallway leading to the tower. And though it should have been, the door wasn't locked, Father Hours trusting parishioners to respect the No Trespassing sign taped to the door. He had no choice. There was no other decision but to follow when his sister said, "Come."

As if pushed, Mary moved down the corridor. Jude stood, uncertain. The fly buzzed against the window. Rain drummed the side of the building. Mary illuminated nothing before, or behind her, but Jude could tell she had traveled about five feet. Pulling the flashlight from a back pocket, Jude flipped its switch, training the beam on Mary. The light, as if swallowed, did nothing. He fanned the light on the floor before him. Narrow wooden planks ran great distances, and the floor looked solid. He did not see any nails or warped beams.

"You're positive they can't hear us?"

"Yes," Mary said. "And do not worry. This bit of floor is safe. I have seen Father Hours and Mother walk this hallway, together. It is only"—she faded—"well, you will see."

No longer dizzy, Jude did not fear injury. Getting hurt. The floor must be solid. Mary had a plan, one that involved Mother, and all would unravel were Jude to accidentally fall, to get injured. His only concern was getting caught, but he believed Mary—there was no way anyone could hear him. Aside from the rain (and even that was muffled) he certainly couldn't hear anything. Confident he could move about undetected, the only issue was …

"Do not worry," Mary said. "No one is looking for you. Mother and Father Hours are at the rectory. Some bishop is coming, and they are getting lunch ready."

"Fine," Jude said. He pointed the flashlight past his sister, flooding the corridor with as much light as the beam allowed. Hugging the wall, he shuffled towards her. Mary continued down the passage, keeping one step ahead of the flashlight. In time, Jude forgot what he was doing.

"Grab the matches," Mary said, stopping.

Jude reached into his pocket for the matchbook, one of many used for lighting candles before mass. He had a bad feeling, but there was no point in lying. Mary knew he grabbed the matches when retrieving the flashlight.

"There is no need to worry," Mary said. "Did you not notice that the room is stone?"

He hadn't. He could no longer hear the rain, either. Walking the corridor was creepy and had occupied his imagination. His footsteps created echoes that reverberated from side to side before dissipating like smoke. Stopping, he had aimed the flashlight overhead, and the result was as he expected. The ceiling was impossibly high, the beam flattening to form a huge circle far above him. The space made no sense.

Mary stood in the center of a circular stone chamber. Strange. There was no smell. Nothing organic or chemical. Yet, and Jude passed the flashlight's beam around the … well, whatever this was.

There were books and chairs. A desk and what looked like a journal. This must be the room Father Hours wanted to show him. Opposite the corridor they had used to enter the space loomed a frame without its door.

"What's in there?" Jude said. Through the passage the darkness was so total as to assume a queer dimension, to become almost bright.

When Mary didn't answer, he turned to face her, mindful to keep the light directed at his feet. She pointed to his right.

"What?" Jude said, turning, and illuminating the area before him.

A stone altar jutted from the wall. Four rows of votive candles rose from this homely chantry, rows symmetrical as stadium seating, each rising to rest one against the other before, ultimately, resting flush against the wall. Jude acted absently, striking matches and lighting every candle, dropping the used sticks in a worn metal cup designed for the purpose. From their gilded sticks the candlelight wavered, aligning along that line where the wall met the ceiling, and from this axis the candles created a semicircle of light, this particular geometry extending a quarter of the way across the ceiling, the candlelight creating a shape as perfect in its symmetry as the setting sun halved by the horizon.

"What now?" He sat on the kneeler.

Jude was disoriented, and he could not determine where they were in relation to the rest of the building. They could be standing over the altar—it made sense—but he wasn't sure. Walking down the dark corridor had messed with his head. Mentally, he placed himself back atop the stairs, by the window, but found, when retracing his steps, that he couldn't, despite knowing that he had seen the lake, determine, with certainty, what direction they had walked. What if the passage was not a straight line? And what did it mean that he occupied a circular space? And what was up with that other opening? Why was there no door? Is that where work was being, or was going to be, done?

"Interesting, no?"

In a way, yes. But, largely, no. Not really. Jude liked reading, but the books did not look interesting. And he certainly didn't care about candles and chairs. What he liked about Church was not up here. Were they in a castle, or some old mansion, he'd think that this room, especially if it were hidden, was cool. But it wasn't atop a castle. The room wasn't even hidden. The space was above a church, and expressly forbidden, but that was only for a boring reason, because the area was under construction. Like an older, much darker, tradition, the room was kind of cool. Although anything was better than waking up every Sunday morning to sit around other people who dressed up and professed to believe in the same God. People, Jude knew, who would never believe in Mary.

"Guess so," Jude said. "But why are we here?"

Back when she was living, Jude never considered Mary being anyone other than Mary. The thought never crossed his mind. She was a leader. Fearless, she loved laughing, and experience, living like a lunatic, trying everything, as if life were a TV whose channels she loved to change, simply because she could. Dead, Mary was more like Mother than Jude had ever dreamed possible. And this realization was weird. And disturbing.

Mother was a pusher. She likened experience to expertise, and had given up, despite some faux affect to seem spirited and fun, trying anything truly new, ignoring all that wasn't in some way associated with organized religion. Everything that she pushed her family to "try"—like a concert, a play, or even eating out—had, for its genesis, Roman Catholicism, and usually stemmed from some association with Our Lady of the Lake. Like a stodgy church bulletin, or any form of social media, Mother, no matter her relationship with a person or cooperating partner, created a dilemma, expecting everyone—particularly her children—to follow her lead. Not for fun. Not because of some spirit associated with adventure. No. According to Mother there was Right, there was Wrong, and she, over time, needed no dictionary to define either.

It was Mother's unchecked faith, and Mary's emerging spirit, that, when combined, illustrated the expanding crack in Jude's understanding of time. Of how things were. Or how things might possibly be. Both Mary and Mother were present. Both moved through the world at the same speed. Mother, not only alive, but totally physically healthy, regressed (or withered) if only by not changing. By questioning nothing that she believed, Mother remained stunted. There was, for her, no hope to grow. Mary, in being dead, seemed to believe in only one thing, and always looked the same.

"What's through that doorway," Jude said.

Mary faded.

Jude moved away from the candles. His eyes adjusted to the darkness. The floor, while solid—the stones, cobbled, and uneven, like those making part of The Commons, were thick—slanted down, and away from the stairwell, the direction from which they had come, and towards the other opening. He was certain that, if he dropped a marble, the glass would roll, and quickly, that the marble would zig and then zag between the rocky crevices until colliding with a wall. While this room was not under construction, the space opposite, whatever was through the doorway, must lead to at least some of what required renovation.

Father Hours, Jude would learn, liked the space because it was unfinished and remained, after all these years, exactly the same. Like a prayer, or a rosary, the tower was something both old and familiar. Something he could hold both within, and without.

Not Jude.

He was uneasy. The space made him uncomfortable. And the feeling had nothing to do with him trespassing. Father Hours wanted to show him the room himself. So there were no secrets. The priest hadn't hidden anything.

Jude's unease stemmed from his sister. The priest, so long as an adult accompanied him, didn't care that he was up here. Jude couldn't figure out what Mary wanted. What it was—like Mother—she was up to.

Still, mostly comfortable, Jude didn't jump when lightning struck—a bright flash, entering the room from behind them and all but erasing Mary—followed by electricity's crazy crack. This room was solid. This room was safe. But what about the other rooms, hallways, and corridors?

Mary stood in the open doorway. She did not call for him. Jude remembered walking The Commons on Christmas Eve before the Freak Accident. How they had been miserable and cold. How—she showed him later that night—Mary's foot was injured, her ankle puffy, her toes turning black and blue. This had contributed to Mary's mood the next morning. Mother ignored Mary because she was excited and didn't want her Christmas ruined. If Mary was okay to open presents, she was okay to sit through mass. Mary, Mother had said, always—

"Did it hurt?"

Jude hadn't expected to speak. He had no intention of revisiting the past. But being up here produced, like a change in temperature, a strange pressure. He couldn't remember what Mary had said, or done, but he could see

Mother. How her face got all ugly when she screamed. And how she reached for the hose from the sink and sprayed Mary in the face, sprayed Mary as she screamed and fell, favoring her sore foot as she scrambled away from the table, Mother storming to the garage and opening the door and apparently not finding what she was looking for and so instead shouting at Mary to go outside, to get outside if she was—

Mary's eyes were so bright. Like staring into the sun, they blinded. And Jude believed that, even as she looked at him, she didn't look to see. That, like some sort of rag doll, she had buttons instead of eyes. He wanted to ask her. Again. He wanted to know what it was like. Being dead. He wanted her to explain everything. What she wanted. Why she was still here.

Or something.

Anything.

But she was only interested in one thing: Mother. And Mary turned. As if carried by a gust of wind she passed through the doorway. Bright white, in the depth of all that darkness, she dissolved, like a snowflake.

Jude did not want to follow.

DECEMBER 29, 1982

They had attended a small gathering at Endwell Funeral Home, where Father Hours had said a few words, and so the Bendz's were late arriving. The family had followed the hearse in the limousine and exited the vehicle behind the cathedral, entering through a side door. They passed Mrs. Kruty. She opened her mouth to speak, but said nothing.

It was snowing. It was freezing. Great wind gusts fell from the sky, flattening the lake's pointed waves. The mourners parked across the street from Cascadilla Lake and, exposed, like soldiers crossing a rice paddy, broke off from the aisle to slide down pews, eyes swiveling, their decisions driven not by attempts to attain any particular sightline or point of vantage, but, rather, to preserve individual, if illusory, states of insulation, feelings of protection created by the fact that their own families remained intact. And how, too, like soldiers, everyone was worried, and jumpy, entertaining their own ideas of dread.

Mother was dressed in black, a slender thread of pearls dark around her pale white neck. Her face, swollen from crying, was blotchy, a field of broken blood vessels. Her eyes, the color of stagnant water, glistened, and her cracked lips pursed. To compensate, she had visited her beautician, had her hair professionally styled, and makeup applied. She looked like a politician.

But what would you have her do?

Ankles crossed, hands folded upon her lap, she sat at the end of the first pew. Her hairspray. Her cloying perfume. Jude, in a navy suit purchased for the occasion, sat beside her. Beside him, Father. To their left, Mary's casket placed on a riser at the end of the aisle, shiny, and blocking the steps fronting the altar.

Mrs. Kruty babysat while Jude's parents had spent a day selecting Mary's casket, funeral plot, and headstone. Jude said he didn't need a babysitter, and argued that he was old enough to be left home, alone. Mother disagreed.

Mrs. Kruty recently had surgery, and, after Jude's parents left, sat on what looked like a doughnut, talking, knitting, and smiling, irritated that Jude had, as a distraction, television. When her medication kicked in, she ushered Jude into the kitchen, pulling from a brown paper bag the ingredients needed to bake chocolate chip cookies. She did not stop talking. Her hands, thick and strong, were liver spotted, coarse veins bulging beneath dry skin fish-belly blue, her yellowed fingernails long and filed into tidy squares. She acted like everything was fine. She acted like one of the nuns from school, telling, and not asking, and forever talking. Jude spoke just enough to seem polite, bothered that Mary didn't appear, that his sister had left him alone with this weird, annoying, person.

When Mother and Father returned, Jude, tired, disinterested in what the adults had to say, slipped into the living room. When, finally, Mary appeared, flashing to life behind the TV, she told him that they couldn't bury her until the spring, that they had to wait until the snow was gone, and the ground was no longer frozen.

"So where are they going to put you?" Jude whispered.

"My body," Mary said, "will be placed on a tray in a freezer in the basement of a mausoleum."

"A what?"

"A big building where they have tombs. You have seen them, at cemeteries."

Jude asked many other questions, but she ignored him.

"They should have just cremated me," Mary said. "They should have donated the money they would have saved, which would have been thousands of dollars, to the SPCA. You have no idea how expensive it is to bury someone. So typical. So dumb."

She faded, and then, "The casket is ugly in the way Mother finds expensive things pretty. Of course she ordered the most expensive object. Cemeteries are for living people, Jude. Mother is better off burying ten thousand dollars. So needless, my internment. Once Mother, Father, and you are dead, where I am buried, and the fact that I am buried, becomes even more pointless. It means nothing. You will see."

The organist pressed a single key and freed four notes, the sound of music waking Jude from his reverie. Listening. Hearing how the slightest sound built in range to become that which was most powerful. While not quite comforting, he welcomed the distraction, his thoughts pivoting.

Maybe Mary was right about all the burying business, but Jude wasn't sure he agreed. At least about the casket. Not so much a color as light itself, an illumination, Mary's casket was impressive. Countless concaves distorted shapes, inverted images, and created shadows. Like a giant clam deep undersea, this vessel, designed for one purpose, was not so much manufactured but carved from purpose, created from worth. As an object, the thing was cool. In shape, the coffin was like one great pill—impossible to swallow.

Jude waited for his sister to appear, to stand beside her casket and tell him what to do, but she didn't. Jude turned in his seat. He had never seen so many people in one place.

Standing room only, mourners took positions against walls and pillars, they leaned beneath stained glass windows and stood, hands clasped, below the cathedral's great domes. It was hot. There were a couple of teenagers, younger kids from school, eyes bright, confused and uncomfortable, sitting close to their parents. There was a man staring at Mary's memorial card, and, heart thudding, Jude recognized him as one of the detectives, the smaller man. Jude turned in his seat, certain that the other, the taller man must be here, too. He pulled into himself and slid lower in his pew.

Mary had resented church, but only church with a lowercase "c." Had she lived longer, she might have grown to loathe organized religion. More likely, she would have come to realize her indifference, hating, for a person like Mary, requiring more effort than she was willing to give. Mary saw in church an extension of Mother. Pointless conformity. Senseless rules. Church, with a capital "C," was, at the time of her death—despite an hour of religious studies every school day—above both twins.

Mostly.

Mother had maintained her belief that Jude was going to make a fine Catholic. She did not omit Mary intentionally. Rather, drawing upon anecdote and intuition, she didn't hold out much hope for her daughter. Unsure, Jude did know that he didn't mind mass nearly as much as Mary, finding in the music alone great peace, a connection with some unnamed something far greater than himself. When the organist moved from Hallelujah into Ave Maria, the song's melody, which Jude had listened to one hundred times before, seemed made, of this exact moment, from his present mood. The organist, a woman, one of mother's friends, sang conversationally, almost casually, until she was no longer singing but simply playing. In time, she made no sound at all. Jude did not know she was crying. He closed his eyes. No one spoke but to whisper, and so, except for those already weeping, or sniffling, the church was filled with the cloistered, those accidental sounds between silences. Creepy.

He imagined the casket—the closed box a long hexagon—and pictured his sister inside, listening. Like a car, the casket was carefully constructed, and he could tell where her head was because the box was shaped like a body, wider at the top where her head rose from her shoulders, her feet pointing towards the altar. When alive, Mary had slept on her stomach, head turned to the side, mouth open. Arms tucked tightly against her sides, the palms of her hands pressed against her thighs, she folded into herself, and, unless it was freezing cold, slept without a blanket. She was funny that way.

Watching movies taught Jude that here, his sister was on her back, her hands, like Mother's, folded on her lap. This bothered him. The church was cold. Outside was freezing, the ground hard as rock. It was going to get warm enough, eventually. The idea of Mary going underground was awful. It was wrong. What if when they buried her, she disappeared completely? What good was having her as a ghost, though? Better that than nothing, but … she would be gone soon. She had to be. He would get older, or she'd get buried and, like that, or for some other reason, she'd disappear. He didn't know how it worked. How Mary worked. He only knew that so long as they kept living this way there would come a time when he would never see her again. Unless he did something. Unless she …

Unaccustomed to crying—he refused, in front of all these people, to cry—his eyes burned, and he had trouble swallowing. It was too hot. There were too many people. Everyone around him looked dizzy. He wanted Mary. He wanted more music.

When, after five, and then ten minutes later, nothing happened, Jude rose. He couldn't take it. Rather than pass

Mother, he slid in front of Father and down the length of the empty pew. The men and women sitting directly behind the Bendzes lowered their heads and followed Jude with their eyes. He rounded the pew and made for the aisle, walking the length of the altar, so halved, taking a step towards the huge, hanging crucifix and crossing the end of Mary's casket, positioning himself as far from Mother as possible.

Father Hours was not leading the service. Beneath a skylight and positioned in a chair off to a side of the sanctuary, he seemed, bathed in a golden shadow, to have fallen asleep, his belly rising and falling. Corpulent, and waxy, the flesh below his neck. Hands drawn within his vestments, a long robe covered his feet. He did not move. He did not open his mouth to speak. Even before Mary died, Jude had not particularly liked him. More than a priest, he resembled Father's barber, Mr. Vinatelli, a man for whom life was a series of simple actions that needed to be completed, and who handed you a lollipop when you were done.

Many of those looking on felt vulnerable. It was one thing to point at Church and laugh when watching TV, at home, alone. It was another to go to mass come Christmas—because it was something like a tradition, if not fun—while making fun of organized religion. Here, these people, surrounded by so much strangeness, felt isolated. Exposed.

Those most uncomfortable were the outsiders. The others. James's colleagues from work. Helen's acquaintances from her time volunteering at the SPCA and the library. People who, when forced to step foot inside a church—to attend a wedding, or a nephew's baptism—felt violated, as though participating in something as spiritual as an abortion.

Not the parents with young children, though. These parents, since learning of Mary's death, confident no similar calamity could again befall such a small community, felt, however guiltily, a sense of relief. Comfortable, embracing the certainty that they were safe, secure from such horrors, they were free to explore, to test the depths of their particular sadness, processing grief in minor registers. Because they were not lost in thought, or prayer, they were the first to notice Jude approaching the casket.

Hunsinger and Vossler, early arrivals, sitting inconspicuously apart, both with clear views of Helen and James, looked. They watched. The wind rattled windows. Dust fell from the ceiling above the altar. The church was drafty. Bundled against the cold, they observed their subjects. The girl's death did seem suspicious, but they did not believe there was going to be much to see. They had asked around. They had done their jobs. Just because a lot of people didn't seem to particularly like the mother? This didn't make her guilty. Even the kids' pediatrician said the mom, while overbearing, was loving. A good person. Sure, anything could go on behind closed doors. But that didn't mean anything did.

Yeah, it was strange that the boy's parents didn't seem to notice, or care, that Jude was hugging the casket. That the kid's face was smashed against the gigantic funeral arrangement. But if a life in lawforce taught him anything, it was that if people acted in any way consistently, it was just that: strangely. Detective Vossler, who had selected a seat closer to the family, leaned back in his pew, peered between the heads and shoulders of the mourners to make sure his partner was looking on, as well. Detective Hunsinger widened his eyes and pursed his lips, and shook his head.

Sad stuff.

But weird, too.

Because Jude didn't mind mass, he came to appreciate boredom. Sunday after Sunday, for as long as he could remember, he sat atop a wooden pew, dressed uncomfortably, separated from his sister by his parents, the ceremony as predictable and as interesting as watching someone button their shirt. While Mary fidgeted, crackling with nervous energy, Jude had turned inward, finding in his boredom a personality, a mental energy he didn't associate with thinking. His thoughts arose not as mere daydreams, but more like the strange, wonderful sorts of scenes his mind conjured while, literally, sleeping. He didn't, like Mary, feel tortured. Or punished. He didn't feel much of anything.

At first, the fact that Mary's funeral was so much like a Sunday, and this down to the way his family positioned themselves in their pew (Jude separated from his sister by Mother), brought about the physical release he associated with boredom. And because Mother had always insisted they leave for mass twenty minutes earlier than necessary (so as to avoid arriving even one moment late), he was accustomed to staring at an empty altar.

Today, though. As, minute after minute, nothing happened, Jude returned, his tenuous grip on reality tightening. Comfortable wearing a tie—Our Lady of the Lake, Boys, imposed a dress code—he had never before worn a blazer. He was hot. Constricted. Sweat from an armpit trickled over his ribs. And, unlike a dream, Mary's casket was right there, all but in front of him, as unusual and as interesting an object as he had ever seen. His mind emptied. He didn't know what to think. For the first time since the minutes and hours following the Freak Accident, Jude was overcome with emotion. Jude was sad. Nauseous, and in pain—as if kicked in the gut—he had stood. Almost mindless, aware only of the detectives, that they would be looking on when he moved, Jude had sidestepped Father, and shuffled down the pew.

The coffin was closed. A framed photograph, a portrait of Mary, taken that fall, rested where her head might be.

Above her torso, lurid as if the coffin were a living organism gashed with a machete, a bright red slash—her funeral spray, dozens upon dozens of roses—erupted like disgorged organs. And above the flowers, as if floating, the word Daughter, flowing in a great, golden script. Jude lifted his sister's picture—he looked nothing like her—and set it by his feet.

Those who had gathered whispered, they alerted, with their elbows and gentle kicks, those yet to notice. Lacking context, the mourners had no means by which to ground their emotions. They were unsure how to feel. What was the boy doing? Shouldn't someone stop him? Do something? Get someone? This wasn't normal. Even those weeping had stopped, straightened, and looked on in shock.

Mary had liked asking questions. Everyone she knew had an opinion. The problem was that everyone liked the sound of their voice too much. They didn't listen. This was one of the reasons why she and Mother hadn't gotten along, and why, as she grew older, they started arguing.

Jude was different.

He felt bad when he asked someone a question and they didn't know the answer. Even worse was watching someone, instead of admitting ignorance, tell a lie. Rather than embarrass someone, or, like Mary, be difficult because she was bored and looking for a cheap thrill, he preferred to explore why people held certain beliefs and opinions, slow to dwell on the subjects that even the adults couldn't explain and didn't understand.

Like Church.

Like how a tiny piece of bread became Jesus' body.

But none of that mattered now—and Jude stepped on the riser supporting his sister's casket. He wrapped his arms around the roses, mashing his head against their soft, moist petals, resting the side of his face against that place where, in his mind's eye, he imagined Mary's.

"Should he be doing that?" someone said.

"This is terrible," moaned another. "Somebody do something."

So long as there have been people, people have pointed to order; people have equated order with beauty. This is because beauty must be organized so that it can be understood; beauty must be reduced to information so that it may be organized. Through his grief Jude disrupted what people expected. In this way, Mary's funeral turned ugly.

"My God," Mrs. Kruty whispered.

Even she, usually so quick to rise, to flutter about, was, like the others, leveled by confusion. By Jude. By a child's body shaking with sobs. By a little boy shaking his head even as his father took him by the shoulders. The mourners squirmed.

Aware only of his grief, of wanting Mary, Jude resisted. Clearing his throat Father had risen, then returned to his seat. He turned and looked at Mrs. Kruty. Snapping from her shock she rose, made for the coffin, and gently placed her hands atop his shoulders. Jude jerked free, shouldering the casket. Mrs. Kruty, centered now, held on to the boy with greater force. The woman's hands on his body were sharp, and heavy. He opened his eyes, but he wouldn't let go. He didn't want to let go. He shouldn't have to let go.

This.

Her casket.

These flowers.

Her picture on the floor.

This, here, was more Mary than some ghost only he could see. And what he felt? For the first time since Mary's first visitation, Jude was not what he thought, but who he was. What, with Mary gone, he had become.

From some part deep inside himself, he registered nothingness. And there, in front of everyone, aware of no one, another piece of himself died. He knew what it was like both living, and being dead. And he understood neither.

And, falling to his knees, his face rose petal red, how he cried for just a little peace to die.

August 10 – 11, 1983

Propped upright in bed, buried beneath a mound of bright white blankets, Jude lay stock-still, thinking about breathing, feeling not the cotton's softness but, rather, the play of the fabric pushing and pulling the hairs on his legs. That his skin was a thing suddenly struck him as interesting, and he ran a finger up and down his arm. Light from the television made the air blue, and, as scene cut to scene, the room shook with shadow.

"Hey there, sweetie," Kilsa said, crossing into the room and stopping before the whiteboard. She erased the name of the day's attending doctor, uncapped a marker with a pop, and wrote another name in its place. "Your night nurse called in, so it looks like you're stuck with me, at least for now."

She reached behind her head and pulled her hair into a ponytail. Lifting the blood pressure cuff from the wall, she loosened the black fabric, the Velcro separating in a sound sudden as static electricity.

Kilsa was pretty. Fit like a jogger, her fingernails polished a light pink, she was always humming and smiling. Jude liked her. She wrapped the cuff around Jude's arm—twice, he was so thin—and, repeatedly squeezing what looked like a black lemon, waited as the contraption, hissing, filled with air. Monitoring Jude's pulse, she took in the TV.

"What's on tonight, kiddo? Anything good?"

"Don't know," Jude said. The sound of his voice surprised him. His throat didn't hurt, but he was thirsty. His mouth was warm and fuzzy. Everything arrived as an echo.

"Careful," Kilsa said. "I might slime you."

Jude smiled. Part of him understood the joke, that she was referencing one of his favorite television shows, and its famous motif.

With a sigh the pressure on his arm released, and Kilsa tore free the cuff and replaced the device. "Purrfect," she said. Moving to the other side of the bed, she pulled the thermometer from its case, dipped the instrument in its well, and, smiling, waited for Jude to open his mouth. It was weird how different these devices were, compared to Dr. Greene's.

"Perfectly usual yet again, Mr. Jude," she said, after checking the reading, tossing the plastic into the trash, and inserting the thermometer into its well.

His parents had just left, after kissing him on the forehead, and wishing him a goodnight. They must be in Father's car, by now. Through the window Jude scanned the roofs of the neighborhood's houses and above these discovered a seagull, fixed like a kite, a point set in the high, blue-bright sky, its wings dipping, angling, and correcting. There were clouds, huge clouds bilious and building from points south and east, gigantic, white, impossible features that pushed him back in place, and how these brought to mind trips to the beach, and how the breeze created a total erasure of sound. What outside this point in time, this room—so sterile and without life, lacking so much as a cloud—could possibly bring him back to this hospital? To the comfort of his honeycomb cocoon?

"How's that IV doing?" She ran a hand over Jude's arm—his scalp tingled—checking the needle, and then the line. He shuddered impossibly pleasantly.

"You comfortable?" She smiled, and fingered the long plastic cord, assessing its slack, measuring his drug drip.

For as well as Jude could see, he was hearing things differently. It was like he had fallen down a deep well, and was looking up at everything, and how, if he looked hard enough, everything was reduced to a small point of light. Thinking about how he spoke, he understood that he was coming across casually, indifferently, as if Kilsa was Mary, back when his sister was alive, and he told her everything.

Always cool, if not cold, hospital rooms are never completely dark, and Kilsa—Jude's favorite nurse—was nice, pretty, and, presently, it was as if she were glowing. He was happy she was with him, that she wasn't going home. Always mysterious, her beauty came in waves that Jude, even when he wasn't sedated, contemplated.

Cloud cover obscured the setting sun, and darkness from the huge picture window erased some of the room's brightness. The window—or, rather, the visions it provided—was a gift, another present inviting a wide breadth of comment, an outlook offering unto Jude something other than the television to consider. Beyond the houses, Endwell's low, rolling hillsides, dark forms like ancient waterlines, interrupted the horizon. A few of these had warning lights, and every evening red lights startled the sky. Every night gave way to morning, and with the sun's watery rise these lights blinked off and into darkness. It was absurd. It was impossible. How the hushed crush of so much meaninglessness had, like dust, settled here, upon this silent and sepulchral space. A reality that Jude realized only as a feeling of security.

Warm, as if his bed were a nest, Kilsa had never appeared prettier; her presence was never more comforting; her body, in outline, a vivid darkness, bright in relief.

But it was more than this. The other nurses had slowed down when interacting with him and, today, they had been short. Today, they had been angry—with him. They made him aware that he was making them work. Worse, he knew that they knew he was faking, and, despite what Mary had told him, he was no longer sure what, exactly, was the right thing to do.

Nervous about who was going to be responsible for running the night's experiment, he was surprised to feel so comfortable, so sleepy, so very at peace. He knew from experience, from overhearing countless conversations, that the night nurses, while never happy to be working all night, took solace in these shifts largely because, given he was in a psych ward for little kids, they could dreamily pass from midnight to morning doing next to nothing. Far worse than making one of them work through the day was creating a disruption at, say, two in the morning. Other than those basic responsibilities hospital administration associated with patient care, Jude demanded nothing. For this reason, Jude was a floor favorite. But, night or day, Kilsa, at her worst, would never make Jude feel badly, or self-conscious.

A voice called across the intercom. High, Jude felt the words, he heard the feeling as something swirling in his belly, and he smiled.

"That's for me, hon," Kilsa said. "I'll be back to check on you. Need anything? You know what to do."

Grabbing a Sprite from the fridge she cracked open the can, and poured the soda into a tall plastic cup.

"You're done with this, right?" Kilsa grabbed the cherry lozenge on the table beside Jude's bed, shiny and red atop a crumpled tissue, tossing the refuse in the trash before Jude had the chance to answer.

"No straw, right?"

And she placed the beverage beside him, offering a backhanded wave on her way out of the room, completely missing Mary's firecracker pop!

Mary waited one minute before speaking.

"Jude," she said. "Jude. Brother. Open your eyes. They are drugging you. I know it is difficult, but you must fight this. Resist. If you fail, you lose. They send you home. Ring that bell and ask for a Coke. Tell them your stomach hurts. You need the caffeine."

Mary, in and out of the room all day, had been quiet, near silent, speaking only twice. Later this evening, and throughout the night, they planned on feeding Jude. Jude, she had said, was going to fall asleep, that he would not be up for making himself puke. They were, she said, going to prove he was not sick. They were, she said, going to send him home. For good.

Jude, happy to be sedated, told her again: he was not worried.

If they forced him to eat, he would force himself to vomit. While this wasn't something he wished to consider, he trusted Mary, completely, and understood that this was a serious situation. He would do what needed to be done. Since his hospitalization, being asleep, or being awake? Jude, more or less, felt the same. Never really tired, and never fully awake, he could—like standing up, or sitting down—do either on command, falling asleep when the nurses turned off the TV and told him it was time for bed, waking, when, in the morning, they flipped on the room's fluorescents. Happy to comply, his existence revolved around answering questions (with Yes or No usually working), on top of whatever his body regulated by way of involuntary action.

Only, strangely, it was growing increasingly difficult to keep his eyes open. And it was like golden sunlight illuminated the insides of his eyelids. And whenever he spoke, or was made to think—or listen to Mary—this gold turned to red and this to violet and purple to green and this to darkness and this alight with swirling chrysanthemum silver bursts, dancing Chinese dragon blasts of mercury sparkling with thin-strung spider-webbed chromatic dimension. Patterns forming only to float. To fall. Stranger still, he felt not as if he were falling, but that gravity had assumed a greater hold of him, and it was no longer possible to move.

Not that he had any interest in moving.

Someone—Jude could not remember who, though it must have been that psychiatrist lady Mother had made him see—told him that people, when they dream, and wake up, terrified, think it was the "monster" that had scared them. But (it was definitely that psychiatrist lady), people had it backwards. It wasn't the "monsters" that were frightening. What really, what truly frightens us? she said. Our dreams.

"Jude," Mary said. "I need to hear you tell me that you understand this is serious. And do not tell me that you know, that you get it, because you do not. What they have put into your body? Your IV? That is not some fluid, Jude. That is not saline. It is lorazepam. It is ketamine. They—"

"Laketawhat?" Jude smiled.

He thought of Kilsa. He looked at Mary. His soda popped and fizzed, the sound roaring like a campfire. He meant to move his eyes, but swung his head, instead. It stopped, with force, against his pillow. Tiny bubbles sprang from the bottom of the cup. How interesting to consider. These were small, one-dimensional bubbles, sliding up a side of the plastic, and then popping. He pictured a pot of boiling water. What if something hot could be cold? He smiled. Weird. The world could be so pretty. It really was terrible that so much of what happened here, on Earth, was ugly.

"Drugs, Jude," Mary said. "Tranquilizers they use on horses, specifically. Not enough to knock you out. But enough so that you will follow the path of least resistance.

This is why you feel so good. So happy. You must free the IV, Jude. You …" Mary pointed at Jude's hand. "It is necessary that you pull that needle from your hand. Otherwise you will eat. You will eat and you will not vomit and you will—"

Jude smiled. He loved his sister. Almost as much as he missed her. But, for once, she was wrong. He was listening to her. He trusted Mary—completely—and he understood that this was a serious situation. He was not worried. He would tell her again. He would tell her again and again and again and again until, finally, for once, she listened. He wasn't sure he could open his mouth, or if his mouth was already open, or if he had just spoken. That, really, was the only problem. While he wasn't cold, at least not exactly, he shivered. Perhaps his body was a breeze …

Mary understood that all was lost, and that it would not be possible to continue punishing Mother in this manner. Jude was going home. For most people, if not everyone, objects appear not in their entirety, but in outline. More accurately, people process places, things, and other people separately, in parts. Jude looked at a television and didn't see a TV. He didn't even see a box. Rather, he processed color. He noted if the object was on or if it was off. Jude had seen people so often and with such regularity to trust, blindly, that when he saw Mary's face, or raised finger, his sister was near … and that she was his sister, completely.

This was not surprising.

This was how the living passed through every waking moment.

Offering unto what they witnessed no affront, no general indignation, accepting the idea of something—or everything—before it had been totally controlled, or contained.

This meant, Mary knew, that Jude wasn't listening.

Mary faded.

Mary knew she was dead because of all the things she could now feel. This way she could now think. There was no new normal. Mary existed, just differently. She was as real as music was real. Still, she lamented not the child—or the daughter—she had been when living, but the person. The human.

With their instruments it is as if musicians slash slits through the fabric of existence. Trios and quartets playing and in their music creating portals through which souls like Mary could pass from one realm into another. Mary did not make this music. Any more than she could make Jude hear. But there was a difference.

Mary looked at Jude.

She thought about Mother.

Both were lost causes. Both, relatively speaking, knew nothing. Yet one would, without seeking, find salvation. Death, Mary knew—and could convince Jude, if necessary—did not hurt very long. And being dead would certainly be better with, than without him.

So strongly was Mary certain of her situation, relative to Jude's condition, that watching him high, with drugs, like warm sugar, running through his veins to leave him feeling blissfully unnecessary, was unacceptable. Her plans for Jude would have to assume what she had known would be their natural form from that first moment when, being dead, she realized she had been murdered. Jude, scared and uncertain, was hopeless. Mary, like Mother, must think of herself. She was no murderer. She was not selfish. But the time for talking was over.

Free now, of Mother, so, too, was Mary's will. Being dead, her decisions were hers alone. Mother was a merchant of misfortune. Mary? An angel of death. But what of it? Forgoing mother's baseless faith, waiting for nothing as make believe as providence, Mary had been given time to right her mother's wrongs.

"Jude," Mary said.

"Hmmmm?"

"You do know that it has been four months since April. You do know that it has been four months since Mother and Father buried me. It does not matter if I am in a tomb. I am going underground. And soon."

This worked. To the degree he was able, Jude straightened.

"I know this is difficult. I heard the doctors, the specialists. Talking to Mother. And Father."

"Really?" Jude said. "Oh, yeah. I mean, I know that. You've told me. Like"—he lowered his eyes, peered at Mary—"you've told me this a bunch of times."

Mary looked different. Less ghost and more … person. When alive, she had never tanned. Whenever they were at the lake, or the shore, she turned pink, before, the next day, as if embarrassed, brightening to become blood red. Less snow white and more human white, flesh-toned, whatever color Mary was – she appeared more real.

"It is just the drugs, Jude," Mary said. "Remove that IV. You will see. Trust me. It is the only way."

"But I like the way you look."

Mary faded. "I do not know how you are feeling, but I know what the drugs are doing. And I know that much of what they are doing is making you feel good. Most of your nurses have supported you. For a long time, though, and I believe you know this, they have not thought that anything is wrong with you. Physically. Or mentally. As such, they do not think you belong."

Jude opened his mouth, and Mary raised a hand. "Let me finish."

Jude smiled.

"Before. Right before Mother and Father left. They spoke with the doctors. With the specialist."

For the first time since the Freak Accident, Mary seemed alive. She was angry.

"They already took the Quarantine sign down from your door."

Jude didn't get the big deal. They would just put it back up.

"No, Jude," Mary said. "They will not. The nurses do not like those men, your doctors, but they agree with them. I told you. This has worked in your favor. They like having you here. You are nice. And easy. They have never lied, but they made sure to make clear that you were in distress." She raised her hand.

"Nothing matters. If you eat, and if you do not vomit. If you—" Mary faded.

"Jude. Listen. Hear me. What is wrong with you cannot be attributed to your body. I already told you. The nurses like you, but they are not your friends. I am not sure why they have not been quick to connect your behavior with Mother killing me. My death. Maybe they have. At least by now. But this does not matter. You must see this. You are in a psychiatric hospital, Jude. This whole time they have been treating your symptoms. Now they are ready to treat the cause."

Jude was trying to listen, to pay attention, but even Mary's words were warm, soft things. Like her breath, each syllable seemed to brush against his eyelids.

"Aside from advising you, there is nothing I can do to help you," Mary said. Light from the television cut into her appearance, and she dimmed, becoming less white and more blue.

"More drugs, Jude. I look different to you because you are being drugged. If you don't remove that needle from your hand, if you do not listen to what I am telling you, they are going to keep drugging you. And when you wake up tomorrow there will be nothing I can do."

"Wake up?" Jude said. "Sure ... but how, Mary? I'm not even asleep."

He pushed against the bed, but his mattress offered no resistance, as if his hands moved through water. Laughing, he lifted his head.

"What's that?" Kilsa said. She entered the room, pushing a tray, stopping at the foot of the bed, and glancing at the TV. "Something funny?"

"Ask for a Coke," Mary said. She moved to stand beneath the TV.

A commercial, a dad sat at the dining room table, an arm wrapped around his young daughter. Beside the young girl her brother looked on, eyeing his sister and then his dad, his face a mask of concern. Before each of them tall glasses of milk-white milk, outrageous in size. The girl, who, on the verge of tears, opened her mouth to speak, stopped, agape, when Mom, appearing from the kitchen, and holding a great bowl of bright red Jell-O, swooped behind the girl, raised and then lowered the dish before her, whispering affectionately into her ear. The Jell-O, an assembly of gleaming red squares, shook like Jell-O squares at a birthday party, but maintained its structural integrity. The girl beamed and leaned into her mother's shoulder.

Kilsa laughed. She checked Jude's drip, pressed, on a machine, a sequence of buttons, and returned to her cart.

The best thing about drugs?

Not only did they make you feel good, but they also presented the absurd—like commercials—in palatable bites that were both silly and seasoned with a blend of logic and reality. Waves of warmth, fuzzy as fur, spread beneath and atop Jude's skin, creating a crisscross of comfort. Only Jude's feet remained cold, as if uncovered. They almost hurt. He almost had enough energy to care.

Mary stared. Her blue eyes bright.

And blue.

For five minutes Kilsa said nothing. Mary watched. For what was so obviously level-headed fairness, even goodness, Mary saw no greater injustice than in saving her brother, than in preserving Jude's well-being. Kilsa did not know Mother. What Kilsa was saving Jude for.

Being dead, Mary did not dislike people—she was indifferent. While confined to the hospital with Jude, it was easy to see that people were drawn to do good. No one was perfect, but those she observed were, innately, good. She saw no one like Mother.

An adult's nature? This was colored more by money and education—those with street smarts were usually the most measured, and compassionate—than anything cosmic. Even though her actions were annoying, Kilsa was a good person. Mary knew this. Still, Kilsa, like Mother, deceived. Waiting, not talking, smoothing Jude's hair, before, almost imperceptibly, lifting the lid from the plate on the tray and, softly humming, pretending to watch the TV, she cut a morsel from a large slice of key lime pie. She hummed. She offered the food to Jude as if he had asked to eat. Mary stared.

Lowering her free hand beneath his chin, Jude, sort of shrugging himself upward, operating from rote memory, from the deep recesses of his drug-addled mind, opened his mouth. The sugar arrived as a heady elixir. The pie struck him like lightning, a jolt in his feet propelling him to, with his shoulders, prop himself upright. Mary stared.

Jude nodded. The sugar was so sweet, and how like a junkie Jude mumbled for more. Kilsa hummed. Leaning from her position to free from the plate more of that which, Mary had told Jude, would, ultimately, seal his fate. Would drive her to take action.

"That's it for now, love."

And Mary stared. She didn't bother speaking. As Jude closed his eyes. As Kilsa, Jude's favorite nurse, wheeled the tray out of his room.

Jude's smiled and closed his eyes. His fate now sealed as tightly as Mary's remains were secured in her tomb.

December 30, 1982

Jude could not move. He was in bed, in his room—where else would he be?—only his mind, like his body, was not working. At least not properly. He called out, but Jude knew he was home, alone, and that he was calling for his mom only to satisfy what his dream demanded from him.

Oh. Okay, then. Well. That explained a few things. He was sleeping. He was having a dream.

Something was wrong. What this was he could not know – he was still dreaming. And to make things worse, the harder he tried to remember, the more he fought to contextualize his feelings, the more his thoughts, like bathwater, spiraled away, lost forever.

Mother arranged his room so that his bed faced the door, enabling her to look in on him, with ease, whenever she pleased. Here, now, his bed had been repositioned, had been turned one-hundred and eighty degrees so that his feet pointed towards the wall, his headboard obscuring him from view. There were windows on either side of him, and the curtains, pulled back and anchored in place, disallowed darkness. And this was a good thing. Because Jude was terrified.

He hesitated, then got out of bed.

Down the hall and into Mary's large, spacious, sparsely furnished bedroom, where countless drawings, sketches, charcoal etchings, and watercolors were, as usual, piled on her dresser, her desk, but no posters, no adornments—their mom saw to this—the bed made, moonlight making bright white lights of her two windows. Over in a corner folded neatly on a chair her school uniform, and beneath the chair her black dress shoes, one set carefully beside the other, the toes scuffed and smudged with dirt. Beside her shoes was her backpack. And everything was dark and swollen with water, water dripping to puddle on her wooden floor. Footprints, their impressions fading, both dark and light, like the full moon's uncertain composition, led from her bed, through her door, and down the hall.

Dressed for mass, Jude understood that his mom was downstairs, and that his dad was in the bathroom, wearing white underwear and a white T-shirt, studying his reflection in the mirror over the sink. He had cut himself, shaving, and blood streamed from a wound in his neck. Light from the bedroom—illuminating, with strange geometry, a widening area of the floor—broke to climb the wall, creating in shape an arrow pointing towards the stairs. Given that it was winter, the house was cold. Breath, like a ghost, rose from his mouth. Everything smelled like pine. Like a giant Christmas tree.

Light as a spirit, Jude entered the kitchen. And in that way of movies, in that way of dreams, the kitchen was filtered with strange, static, flashbulb-white light, and Jude watched himself at the kitchen table, sitting, waiting, and there was his dad, and there was Mary in her red pajamas, complaining about going to mass, about how her foot hurt and was swollen, and how, if Mom would only look, she would see that her foot was black, too, and that she probably had frostbite from walking all over Endwell before, while getting pounded with snow and whipped by wind, standing to stare at some living nativity.

There was a sound. He watched himself sitting on the sofa. He watched the tall detective walk in and stop in front of their Christmas tree. The man was interested in their presents; he reached forward and almost touched an ornament. As if frightened, he stopped. Someone had unplugged the lights, but the sun, streaming from the kitchen, illuminated the tinsel and made bright many of the bulbs. The short detective was saying something to Father. Father nodded. He cleared his throat. Mother was angry. Mary was not there.

Unsure what happened—Jude wished he had been paying attention—Mary and Mom were shouting. He wanted to speak. He wanted Dad to say, to do something. But maybe he, like Jude, was shocked. Or perhaps Jude, unlike his dad, refused to grow accustomed to Mom and Mary fighting.

Mom's face got all ugly when she screamed. She farted with her face, Mary said, when Mom was unhappy, and this had always made Jude laugh. Ordinarily, seeing Mom "farting with her face" got him to smiling, only something different had happened. And this wasn't funny. Mom had the sink's hose and, tracking Mary as she scrambled from the table, she sprayed his sister in the face, and then, when she turned, soaked the back of her head. Water was everywhere. Mary, favoring her foot (it wasn't frostbite, but it was sore, and swollen), had fallen to the floor. Mom had turned and made for the garage. She returned, empty handed, angry, and surprised. With herself. With all that had happened. Wasn't this Christmas morning? Wasn't Christmas morning supposed to be lovely? If only Mary had remained silent. If only Mary hadn't been so interested in arguing.

In the beginning, Mary refused to open the door. The deck was white and formless and empty, a sparkling snow blanket many feet deep, and the low gray sky hovered above it all.

"Get outside," Mom said, unlocking and snapping open the door. "Right now."

Mary saw the snow, and she separated the snow from the coldness. Mom called Mary "ungrateful," and her behavior "unacceptable." Mom said that Mary should shut up, that she might as well stop talking, for she had ruined the morning, and for that she was going outside, and there was nothing she could do, or say, about this.

Mary said, "But I'm soaking wet! I'm in my pajamas!"

Angry, Mom closed her eyes. And then she opened them. "Open your mouth again," she said, "and you'll be in your underwear."

For one moment there was inside, and there was outside, and what separated Mary was a thick plate of glass.

Mom said, "Cool off for a bit, and then we'll see how you feel."

Mary wept. Mary called her mom "unfair," and screamed, saying that she would "freeze to death."

And Mom seemed to think this was good. She said, "I don't care if it's your birthday or Christmas day. That's just not how you speak to your mother. No how. No way."

And it was terrible the way she spoke. And like a fist the wind fell from the sky and slapped the side of their house, and their mom left the kitchen, she returned with four or five towels. And when the floor was dry she tossed the towels next to the door leading to the garage, and she created a large pile for the floor was very wet.

She said, "James, honey? Please take Jude upstairs." And then to Jude, smiling, she said, "Teeth, Jude. And wash your face." She eyed her son. "I'll be up in a minute, after I take care of things down here." She frowned, then said, "And Jude, don't look at me like that. Your sister will be just fine."

Only this was not so.

Their mom didn't mean to kill Mary. But Mom had lost her temper. She had gone too far. She didn't know it, yet. But—and it didn't matter that Jude wanted to stop, that he wanted to scream (he watched himself follow his dad from the kitchen and through the living room)—she would find out soon.

Mom said, "Let's see what Mary has to say after this."

She cleared the dishes from the counter, and the dishes from the table. And she filled the dishwasher, she freed the detergent from beneath the sink, and she poured the Irish green snowflake-sparkling granules into the back of the open door. After shutting the trap, she closed the door and started the machine, stepping from the kitchen when, with an audible click, the dishwasher kicked to life.

Mom said, "What are you looking at?"

And Jude was surprised, not because he was upstairs, but because he didn't think he was visible, that he was seen.

Jude said, "Nothing."

So Mom punished Mary. In her anger and in her rage she punished Mary in the only way she knew how. One she believed to have been born out of love for her daughter. Twisted logic that killed Mary.

This is the truth.

The tragedy is that the truth was not a part of Mom's intended lesson. This was not part of her plan.

Jude was no longer sleeping. He, in bed, was very much awake. Moonlight, made brighter by the fallen snow, lit his room an unwelcome white. He was uncomfortable. Tired. In this liminal state Jude desperately wished for rest, for more time, that his day was ending, not beginning … for to be awake was to be terrified.

Although he didn't complain, Jude simply didn't want to move. For days now he remained exhausted, half-understanding what was happening, or why. He needed sleep. Only—as if truly haunted—all Jude felt was fear. All any new day offered was dread. There was nothing to fear, not that he knew of, but Jude was afraid. Afraid not of

Mary, but that she was the only person he could talk to, Jude, terrified that he was not in control, was a dark star, fixed in time and space.

Human beings experience many problems and endure much pain. It is one thing when pain is the result of recognition, of the awareness that we are not what we would like to be. But Jude was still a boy. A child. While obvious that the world, with or without Mary, would exist, it was just as obvious that there was something very—very—wrong with the world. Anyone could see this.

But if this was all Jude could know, what, now, to make of his existence? From the beginning, then, Jude's eyes were directed toward the dead.

From her first apparition, Mary had been wrong. Jude was listening. Jude had tried to tell her, too! He wasn't courageous, or brave, because there was no reason to be afraid. But now, in the absence of her ghost, he was terrified. She had sounded smarter, like Father. But, like Mother, she sounded defensive, too. More annoying, when she didn't know the answer to a question she wouldn't say, "I don't know."

No.

Just like Mother she would change the subject.

Yes, for all her visiting, Mary ignored … That, or she failed to listen to him, too.

From the sky and through the trees behind their home the wind fell and, like a current within a river, flattened against their home, and the walls shuddered, dust falling from the ceiling, tiny particles brighter than his room. Jude didn't know if Mary was dead or if she was alive when Father pulled her into the kitchen. Later that night Jude had asked her, but she either didn't know, or wouldn't say. He figured she was dead if only because she didn't look alive, her face light blue, and her lips even bluer – like she had been sucking on a blue raspberry Blow Pop.

At the most basic level, Jude could learn that wind is created as a result from differences in the Earth's temperature. But no one, not even Father Hours, could explain why. As in: why there are molecules to begin with. Or who had made them. Mother didn't disregard so much as dismiss science. Said God was miraculous, and worked in mysterious ways. But how could Jude believe this, when she lied about everything else?

And Mary was not much different. She could tell Jude how she was dead, and why, but that was all—or so it seemed. What Jude couldn't figure out was where she had been yesterday, why she had left him alone with her body, in that coffin. Did her dead body make being dead, at least around him, impossible? She wasn't here to reveal secrets, she had said, but to expose the truth. Was her body a barrier, then? She wasn't a secret, she had said. Okay, then. Well then how come he was the only one who believed enough to see?

"Mary," Jude said.

Mary did not respond.

"Where were you?"

When Mary appeared, she did not blink. She did not move. Like Jude's bedroom, she simply was. Organized. Arranged.

Jude had not admitted this—and he never would—but he believed in prayer. People fought too much about things they didn't understand. He didn't think that the wind came from God, as a prayer came from a person. But he did think that if you thought back far enough, you reached a point where you couldn't explain something that created something. At this point he got dizzy. His mind blanked, and he stopped thinking. What he believed wasn't something conjured from guilt or fear. When Jude prayed, he believed. He didn't believe in God, like little kids believed in Santa. No. For Jude, God was a part of Jude— the best parts of Jude.

He knew he was just a kid. That there was a lot he didn't know. Prayer was simply a way of asking more from himself. Only he could produce change. And that which he couldn't change, only he could control how he felt—and how he would allow those feelings to drive his actions.

But there had to be another way of thinking.

There had to be.

Like he saw on Ripley's. An episode where people were doing things with their brains. Like making objects move. Or bending metal objects, like spoons. Someone, Jude couldn't remember who, suggested that we didn't make, or even have thoughts. The person, probably a priest from another parish, suggested it might be possible that thought, or prayer, didn't come from us, but just was. His position, which was more of a question, was that we used our brains to enter into ideas. And so, when praying, we weren't sending ourselves out to God, we were joining Him. Jude had liked that. The idea of setting his soul free.

Eyes closed, Jude actively looked at the back of his eyelids, and here, where there was greater darkness, he prayed for Mary, Jude prayed for his sister to appear. No longer interested in his dream, Jude peered and, hands folded atop his chest, prayed. Operating more from fear than love, Jude, in accepting his sister as deity (she wasn't some ghost, or, to take one of her many words, ghoul) did not want to feel better as in okay. He wanted to feel calm, certain that, after everything that had happened (Mary had appeared every day since being dead), it was impossible to be nothing. He wanted to be able to summon her. If she came when he called, Jude knew that he would be able to hold her. That she would be more than mere apparition. That Mary, while still a ghost, would not be something that he would simply pass through. Like fog, or mist.

Jude was not sure. Did the pop! occur when, feeling as though he was falling through his bed, Jude opened his eyes?

Or had Mary, when taking shape beside his alarm clock's stark red glow, jolted him from his reverie? Not that it mattered. She was here. Like God, she had answered his prayer.

Being dead, Mary looked dead. Nothing about her suggested life. Or living. But her hair, long and curly, was dry. And she was in no way blue. Just white. And so white that her blue eyes, so blue before she had died, seemed even more dazzling, more alive.

"You heard," Jude said. It was very early in the morning. His room was dark. "You came."

"I came," Mary said. "But not because I heard anything."

Jude closed his eyes.

Opened them.

"But I was praying," Jude said. "I was looking, really looking! And I was praying and you … you appeared. You're here."

"I am here," Mary said. "But Jude. There is no such thing as prayer. It is not as though one plus one equals two. That is just math. Those are just numbers. Something people made up. A concept. An idea."

Jude was too happy to argue, to bother figuring out what she was trying to say. Just because Mary was dead didn't mean she knew everything. He wanted to get up from bed and hug her. This seemed impossible, but calling for her, praying for her and expecting her to appear? That had seemed impossible, too. So maybe …

"Come," Mary said.

Get up? Follow Mary? This didn't seem possible. This didn't seem like a good idea. At all.

"Don't worry about Mother, if that's what you're worried about," Mary said. "She is sleeping."

"But what if she wakes up?" Jude said, shedding his covers and getting out of bed.

"She will not," Mary said. "She takes drugs to help her sleep. You would have a hard time waking her if you wanted to. Get dressed."

"Where are we going?"

"Where you have been," Mary said. And, like smoke moved by a gentle breeze, she turned, and made for the door.

Jude sighed. He knew there was no way to touch her.

The sky was completely clear, the moon directly overhead. It was very cold, but Jude had put on his snowsuit and boots. He was not surprised to come upon the pond. Since crossing the hedgerow, the air carried, however faint, the fungal aroma of rotten produce, a stench of death and decay that had nothing to do with humanity. From a distance, hiking up a bit of a hill, the pond was less an opening within the earth's surface than something deposited upon it, a pile of crushed stones, moonlit, minerals glittering. Jude was curious.

Cresting the hill, the smell grew stronger, and, making its summit, the pond presented itself in outline. The pond had not completely frozen over. Tiny patterns like oil swirled upon the surface of the still water. Only there were no patterns; what existed, Jude created. When Jude stopped walking, nothing swirled. It had only looked that way.

Bubbles broke the water's plane somewhere near its center. Somewhere near its center because the pond was not circular, it possessed no named shape. Was it possible for something to lack a center? Breath escaped Jude's mouth. The air was still like the water. The snow-covered fields sparkled and glittered, windswept surfaces perfectly smooth.

The bubbles issued forth like there was a fountain placed beneath the surface. It was probably a snapping turtle.

"Make a snowball," Mary said.

"Huh?"

Mary stood by the water. She remained motionless. Whiter than the snow, Mary was compact, complete. Her eyes were bright and blue, and while Jude knew that she wasn't, that it was not possible, she, in substance, brought to mind something solid. Something as hard as bright blue … ice.

"Make a snowball."

Jude stooped and fashioned a snowball. Cold registered through his gloves. "Okay. And?"

"Throw it."

Jude grew excited. If the snowball hit Mary? If the snowball didn't just pass on through? Everything would change. It was stupid, it wasn't like he could hurt her, but still, Jude didn't want to do something rude, like hit her in the face. Turning, he took a few steps closer, and eyed her shoulder. He took a breath and—

"Not at me, Jude," Mary said. She flickered. Or it may have been a trick of the light, as a cloud slowly crossed the moon. The stars in the sky were very bright. They looked tiny, as if they were moving—as if they were falling—further away from the Earth. "Throw the snowball in the pond."

The pond? For real? Whatever. Angry, Jude threw the snowball, expecting to clear the pond completely. Not. Even. Close. The snowball dropped through the water with a protracted plunk. The bubbles stopped. A few moments later the bubbles reappeared, further from shore.

"If you had not thrown that snowball," Mary said, "the bubbles would not be here."

Jude didn't know what to say.

"By which I mean there."

Jude lowered his head.

"Do you remember the last time we were here?"

Jude opened his mouth to speak—of course he remembered—but then closed it. They had been here countless times, and recently, too. Mother never let them go ice skating, but they played atop the ice anyway, working to see through what they called "glass" for signs of life they knew existed only when the surface of the water had been "sealed."

"Think," Mary said.

Jude stared across the water. What came to mind was not two weeks or even two months ago, but some point last summer. The afternoon had been incredibly hot. There was nothing by way of sound to distract them; even that which moved, moved silently. There was an animal not far from where they sat, and the creature slid into the pond. The algae was thick and green and moved like a wrinkle in a sheet. A snake. The creature crossed the water. The green slime parted into heavy gullies. Jude remembered closing his eyes. When he opened them he could no longer see the snake.

Cattails rose from the shallows. A slow trickle of water fed into the pond from a drainage ditch. Here, the water ran black and clear, and water lilies lay upon the surface like napkins on a table inside a fancy restaurant. Over there, blue water lily flowers, their long pedicels erect above the water, radiant, the tips of so many candle flames.

Beside Mary—with her resting smirk and soaring soul—Jude experienced elation. There was nowhere else he would rather be. Dragonflies dipped and skimmed the water. Hovering, rising and falling, suspended in air, movements impossible, and in these creatures and in their movements, there was no great mystery. There was no reason to wonder. To think.

A log broke the surface of the water. That place where, come mid-morning, turtles basked in the sunlight. A frog rose to the surface; sunlight made black spectral points of its rounded eyes. The frog sank beneath the algae. Directly across the water there was a heron. Sleek and graceful, it was impossible to determine if the bird was asleep or awake.

Tall grasses bent, they swayed with the gentle breeze, and petals from some nearby tree fell upon the water's surface. Such simple cause and effect. Jude felt a little dizzy. Why didn't he faint? Jude had closed his eyes; the world remained. Not as it had been, but how it was. When Jude opened his eyes, things were exactly the same.

A mosquito bit his arm and began drawing blood. Slowly, very slowly, Jude moved his finger several inches forward, and from side to side. Jude brushed the mosquito. Jude had not intended to injure the bug. The bug died. Squashed, its guts, mixed with his blood, smeared across his arm. There was a lot more blood than Jude expected. Much of the blood was his, he supposed. In color closer to black, to crimson, the petals of a dead geranium ... there was a lot of blood.

Jude turned from the pond, he left his reverie. From here, so high atop the hills, with the trees free of leaves it was possible to see Endwell Community College. And how the campus looked as dark and silent as a cemetery, a series of stark, base shadows black against the austere rise of the distant hillsides. Iridescent lights sparkled bug-zapper blue above the sidewalks of roadways and the sidelines of athletic fields and from within that deep solitary darkness glittered as if planets from some distant galaxy. Light posts lined the empty streets and light posts illuminated the empty parking lots and together they worked to form a pattern like that of some unknown constellation. Some of them like collapsing stars blinking on and off and then back on again. On and off and then back on again. A fixture eradicated only by the risen sun.

And of course, Cascadilla Lake, opposite the direction from which he had come. When there is a moon the lake glows deep blue, a hue that brings to mind the stained glass windows inside Our Lady of the Lake. And like the amount of direct sunlight determines the degree of blueness that defines the defeated form of a crucified Christ; whether it is a cyan or a periwinkle blue that makes a mournful Mary; the position and phase of the moon have a similar effect upon the blueness of Cascadilla Lake. A full moon, like now, and the water shimmers the powder blue of the Virgin Mary's cloak. A crescent moon, waning, low over the city's south side, and the lake is that same sapphire as the ridges of those bruised ribs in outline atop the Son of God's pierced, emaciated, abdomen.

But even when the moon is new you can see the water. Even when clouds mask the moon you know the lake is there. Only the water isn't blue. The water is black. Much blacker than the skyline, and made even darker by Endwell's twinkling lights, whose streetlights, gold as the flames of votive candles, run in neat, parallel lines across the city; and whose house lights, dazzling as the wings of fairies, lay scattered in various degrees of concentration around the blackened body of water. The pitch of unreflected light, Cascadilla Lake seems to descend into that swath of eroding earth with the same dizzying speed of the black expansion of nightfall bleeding into space. That place Jude still considered heaven.

"Why did you bring me here?" Jude said. He was cold, and shivering, but he was not ready to return home.

Mary flickered. Overhead, as if evaporating, the sky's few clouds had disappeared.

"If you are to be able to see me, I need to know that you will follow me. That you will do as I say without questioning."

"So this was like a—"

"Without questioning."

And Mary, like snow carried by the wind, made for their house.

And Jude, as if directed to do so, followed.

March 25, 1983

The psychiatrist wore a white turtleneck. Over this a white coat, the type actors wore when playing doctors, on TV. Accustomed only to seeing her head poking up from a pew, Jude was far more interested in her appearance than anything she had to say. Here was a woman without definite shape. In brown corduroys, wool socks, and Birkenstocks, she was a series of slashes and crazed angles, the side of her neck and jawline scarred, but not terribly, her skin, instead of white, a taut pink pocked. She was very pretty (even Jude was curious to see where her scars ended), only she looked tired, as if she were missing a dimension, as though too much experience had erased a once lovely quality. Her thinness was a challenge, one that suggested she labored to control a stillborn fury. To see her was to know, instantly, that she would be just as likely to laugh as to scream.

Shrinks.

Jude saw them coming a mile away.

This one, though. On her jacket glittered a small, gold, pin. A crucifix. Even minus the adornment it was evident God played a significant role in this woman's life's decisions. Obviously. Why else would Jude be here? Mother's circle, while seemingly large, was, in reality, as tight as skin on a fist.

Like anyone strongly associated with Our Lady of the Lake, Dr. Vicki helped the other parishioners, who, like married couples, grew to look like one another. These were men and women who resembled each other not in face or feature but in the way that members of a guild look similar; how a group of peers share a certain way of resting on a chair; of speaking with their hands ... of, more than anything, smiling.

Jude processed the room's silence before realizing the woman had spoken to him. School-aged children, most with their moms, filled the nearby seats. Two plump women with big hair sat behind the large wooden desk opposite the front door, answering the phones, entering data into their computers, and chewing gum. To his left a huge picture window. Jude watched it snow. Fat, lazy flakes fell to the Earth like petrified ash, melting when landing on cars, disintegrating when striking the concrete, white as Mary against swathes of early spring's dark green grass. The space smelled like kitty litter. Of poverty. Jude had a scratch on his index finger, the dried blood thick like a candle's melted, reformed, wax.

"Knock, knock," Dr. Vicki said. "Anybody home?" She leaned forward, made a fist, and, smiling, rapped the air a few feet in front of Jude's face.

He should have stayed in the bathroom. Gross as it was, at least the woman wouldn't have found him.

"You ready there, mister?"

Jude wanted to say no. He wanted to say fuck you. It would be so cool to jolt one of these adults awake from security and into uncertainty. To shock them into a shuddering sense of self-doubt. To make them walk around with questions instead of, smiling, and self-satisfied, their opinions. Their certainty.

And this much was true: he could say anything.

He could say, no.

He could say, fuck you.

Because what he said did not matter. It wasn't like she was going to leave him alone. So why, then, the need to make it easy? Besides. Where was Mary? Jude had no idea what he was doing. Dr. Vicki wasn't here to help him. Not really. She wanted to impress God. And, if not Him, well, then, in her estimation, the next best thing: Mother. Since the Freak Accident, this appointment, more than anything Mother had asked him to do, or had told him he was going to do (other than returning to school), Jude had feared. Which, owing that his baseline was terror, made the prospect particularly horrifying. Mary had explained what psychiatrists did, but Jude wasn't sure what psychiatry was, what Mother wanted from him. One thing he did know? And he stood from his seat. He didn't want to talk about his feelings. With anyone. Let alone some weird woman from church.

But he also knew that he didn't have it in him. Being mean. Acting anything other than polite. Life would certainly be easier if he did. Life would be much easier were he more like Mary. But he didn't. And he wasn't.

Jude waited while Dr. Vicki unlocked a door. He followed, in silence, as they walked down a corridor. He didn't care what other people thought about him; he cared how other people felt. The thought of other people being sad was enough to make him uncomfortable to the degree that he would put others' happiness before his own. More than his own well-being, he didn't want other people feeling badly. And this was something that no one, not even Mary, could ever understand.

The afternoon was still. Sounds entered the office with effort, the space a tidy tomb. Someone was vacuuming the hallway. The machine came close to, and then receded from, the shut door. For a moment its hum swallowed all other sound. Dr. Vicki smiled. She waited. Impatient. Irritated. There was a window behind her desk. The sky transformed. Thin, low-hanging clouds moved quickly, their shadows shrouding the earth. The gray sky contracted, becoming black, and then the heavy noise of raindrops drumming the hoods and roofs of those cars parked in the lot. And the roof, directly overhead. And the rainfall, mixing with the snowflakes—thicker now, fat as field mice—was as brief as it was dramatic.

"I'd like to read from St. Anne," the psychiatrist raised an index card. She stared at the door. "St. Anne is glorious among the Saints not only because she is Mary's mother, but also because she gave Mary to God. The number of cures wrought through the inter—"

Dr. Vicki had a nice voice. She read without embellishment, but with rehearsed refinement, so the words, unfamiliar as they were, possessed a strong cadence, a peculiar intercession. Jude relaxed. His mind wandered. The sun was shining. Reflected light made the world seem brighter. Jude listened. He tuned in. Not to what the lady was saying, but to the sound of her voice.

We, being people, expect happiness. In truth, we should be amazed that happiness bothers to enter existence at all.

Jude was happy. Relatively.

"You know, Jude," Dr. Vicki said. Pausing, she held a tissue to her nose. Her nose was very red and swollen— almost radiant. "Most children who have, or who experience nightmares, think it's the 'monster' they're afraid of. Really, though"—and she lowered the tissue, and held it, crumpled, on her lap—"it's our dreams that scare us. The monster is just there to remind us of something."

Jude nodded. He hadn't realized she had moved on from whatever prayer she had been reading and was talking about dreams, noting how it's important to not only listen to what our dreams tell us, but how we can ask dreams to do things. Like most words coming out of the mouths of most adults, Jude had no idea what she was talking about.

Still smiling, she rose and walked over to a corner of her office. Like the bathroom, only ten times as big, the space was depressing. The overhead light made everything look sick, and yellow, and wrong—anything even close to yellow in color becoming brown. The door was thick, constructed from cheap, heavy wood, its paint chipped, its base blackened and scuffed.

Still, Dr. Vicki brightened her office with small, personal effects, understanding class and understatement in ways that suggested another way of life, that promised this iteration of Dr. Vicki, professional or otherwise, was a woman who had only recently found Christ. On her walls there was nothing like you'd see inside Mother's friends' homes. No crosses. No pretty Jesus Christs glossy like models and, somewhat smirking, palm raised, centered within gaudy golden frames.

But she was one of them, now; she had been double dipped.

There was no doubting that.

Like a Born Again on a blind date she shot glances over her shoulder, nervous, ever-smiling, as if Jude might get up from his seat and what? Scream? Faint? Touch her? Vomit? Like pretty much everyone from Our Lady of the Lake, the woman was pure whacko.

Jude had always, however subconsciously, associated poor people with what Mother called sinning. And sinning was depressing. Maybe it wasn't all that depressing, though, being in this office. At least he wasn't in the waiting room. And the bathroom? With its dirty toilet and piss-yellow urinal cake? Petrified and assuming, in shape, an old snowball? Gross. How could a place like this have, for kids like him, a room like that? Entering the bathroom was like stepping inside of a smell. How anyone …

A fly rose from the windowsill, climbed the pane, then loped about the room. A dark contrast against the light, Dr. Vicki raised a hand as the insect passed her head. Returning, she centered an expensive-looking chess board on her glass coffee table. The psychiatrist took her seat before white.

Jude knew—Mary had told him—that chess was Dr. Vicki's way of befriending her patients while, simultaneously, distracting them. She added that Mother told Dr. Vicki that Father had taught Jude how to play, and chess was his favorite game. Jude nodded. This was true.

"You okay?" Dr. Vicki said.

Puzzled, Jude didn't know what to say. Then he remembered: body language was a language, one that people like Dr. Vicki constantly read.

The fly buzzed around the room, returned to the window, smacked against the glass, and fell. The insect, flat on its back, buzzed, and then stopped. Her office quiet, Dr. Vicki smiled, and, without speaking, opened the game.

Interesting. She played differently than Father.

Jude processed, more than understood the pop!, the way that not only light, but that pressure, the air in the room, changed when his sister appeared. Dr. Vicki didn't notice. Jude was a bit disappointed. He'd wondered if anyone else could see his sister, maybe this sort of doctor could.

Mary stood in front of the psychiatrist's computer. Made almost invisible by the great white light that passed through the window—reducing his sister to bright blue eyes and rich brown hair—she raised a finger to her lips. Behind her, the fly, as if bothered by Mary's presence, worked its way up the glass. As if it could possibly escape.

The room was warm. A bead of sweat slid down a thigh, and Jude flashed to Mary's funeral, he saw her strange, underwater box gleaming before the altar. He remained motionless. He would move when the fly moved. A good plan, he thought. It made a certain sort of sense.

Mary lowered her finger. She nodded, yes.

Dr. Vicki was telling the truth. Usually, when responding, Jude was noncommittal. The other night, following another nightmare and finding Mother at his bedside, he had admitted that he was afraid of school. He didn't tell Mother exactly why, just that he was. So it was natural for her to draw conclusions. Here? Now? Jude did not want to make a similar mistake.

Through the window the parking lot glistened. The asphalt dipped to inform a narrow ravine defined by symmetrical plots of meticulously mowed turf, the grass heavy with green, encapsulated within long ovals of concrete curbing, urban architecture created to slow those cars intent on using the lot as a passing lane. Jude couldn't see her station wagon, but Mother was no doubt near. She probably sat in her car in that spot where she had pulled to a stop, parked, and walked Jude inside.

The clouds broke. The fly skittered up and across the glass before taking flight, streaking across the room, and striking a light fixed to the ceiling.

"Everything alright?" Dr. Vicki said.

Jude nodded. Leaning forward, he countered her move, then sat back in his seat.

Irrelevant, what Dr. Vicki said, given that Mary insisted Jude say nothing. To come across nice, or polite—he looked at Mary, who, as usual, did nothing—she said it was okay for him to use his body. That it was okay for him to nod. To shrug. But absolutely no talking. Fine by Jude. Even though Dr. Vicki was kind, and probably even good (at least she wasn't creepy, like so many of the other people from Our Lady of the Lake), it didn't matter what she did … Jude couldn't mention Mary. And so everything he said was going to be misinterpreted. Even if the sentiments he expressed as fact were accurate, the truth of all this would be erased by those boundaries Mary had put in place. Plus, he and the doctor were separated by a whole lot of religion.

"So. Your mom tells me that you've been having trouble sleeping. She also mentioned"—Dr. Vicki advanced a pawn—"that you hate school."

Jude shrugged. This was true.

"Actually"—Dr. Vicki blew her nose—"she said you are scared. No. What she actually said, if I remember this right, is that you are frightened of school. Afraid."

An inlet to Cascadilla Lake edged one end of the parking lot. Stagnant firth. Tepid channel. Across the way a row of weeping willows—their showy branches making shadowy tunnels; their fallen leaves still upon the fusty water—and between the parking lot and rotting water a beveled length of weathered grass. Despite the cold, old men sat atop white buckets, their fishing poles resting in the forks of thick branches screwed into the deadpan earth. Paint-splattered Salvation Army slacks. Plastic sneakers missing shoelaces. Forty-ounce mouths rose from brown paper bags limp as the catfish and carp these men pulled from this toxic tributary. Eyes yellow and heavy— red veins thick and bulbous, a web of forgotten thought— the men slowly blinked as Mother drove past. It stunk. A stink that filtered into, and through, the car. Like compost.

"I wonder if Dr. Vicki knows about all of this," Mother had said.

Knew of what, exactly, Jude wasn't sure. But he had an idea. He had thought of the pond by their house. What Mary had said.

The fly, still above them, gripping the light, rotated three-hundred and sixty degrees, and then flew off, landing on the doorknob.

Dr. Vicki, while she wasn't as good as Father—who, when he wanted to joke around, knew at least seven ways to checkmate Jude in eight moves or less—was good. Able to think a couple moves in advance himself, Jude didn't return his knight but kept a finger atop the piece when Dr. Vicki, after making a strange vocalization, leaned forward in her seat. Jude did not suffer from pride. He wanted to learn. The psychiatrist smiled and leaned back in her seat as Jude reconsidered. Seeing his mistake, he defended, rather than attacked. He would have smiled, were Mary not in the room.

"You know, Jude," she said, considering the board. "Anything you say here? Anything at all?" She advanced a bishop. "It stays between us. Strictly. Even if I wanted to tell your mom. Even if I thought I should tell your mom?" She brought the tissue to her nose. "Well, I couldn't. It's illegal. If anyone found out I would get … well, I would lose my license. My job. And I love my job. The work I do here."

Jude didn't like when people used his name in sentences. To hear his name was like a slap across the face—an action, more than a word.

Jude was not like Mother.

He did not like attention.

Anyways. Jude didn't know about all of that. But her line of questioning? Well, using his name or not, she was telling the truth. The other night he had made a mistake, admitting (he must have been mostly asleep), that he was afraid of school. Mother comforted him, but she bugged him about it, the what he was afraid of, all morning, and then on through the rest of the week. Jude said nothing. Which was why he was here.

Jude looked up from the board. Mary, ghostly, made all but invisible by the bright white light passing through the window, raised a finger to her lips and shook her head. She had prepared him for this. Had said that, with Mother, he had used emotional language. That he had opened up, that he had given the adults something to seize, words that they could mold to make meaning. Jude wasn't sure he agreed until Dr. Vicki acted like a psychiatrist, her jump from "hate" to "fear" unnerving.

"I hear you like music?"

Jude nodded. He reasoned this was okay. He reasoned wrong. Mary flashed. A crazed lightning bug blue. Jude flinched. Dr. Vicki turned and faced Mary.

"Well prayer is certainly an instrument that makes beautiful music," she said, facing Jude. Smiling. She freed and brought a tissue—the second, Jude noted—to her nose.

The fly, circling the room, made for the window, buzzing, returning overhead, before smacking against the glass. Dr. Vicki nodded when Jude moved a pawn, effectively securing a position.

"At least in a manner of thinking?" She advanced a pawn to meet his. "Prayer must seem pretty strange to a young man your age. I mean, even I didn't always know that God, that Jesus Christ lived inside my heart. Had a place inside me. But I found it helps to think like this—"

She paused for effect.

Jude made sure she knew that he was listening; he met her gaze.

"The thing with prayer," she went on, dabbing her nose. "Well, so many people think, in a way, that prayer changes God. But, well, that's not really the case. That"—she reached for tissue number three—"well, that's impossible, right? God is God and will forever be God. Like Love. But the power of prayer is that it changes us. It changes those of us who do pray. And this, at least I think so …" and she reached for an index card on a corner of her desk, all but brushing against Mary.

Had an arm passed through her?

Jude didn't think so.

"This is why we listen to music. Why we listen to music when we want to feel good, and maybe dance." She read the card—it was obvious many of these words were not her own—and then, keeping her eyes on Jude, returned the card to her desk. "Or to celebrate something, like a wedding. Or maybe when we're sad, like at a funeral."

She let the word funeral, which she all but spit, enunciating each syllable as if it were its own word, part of a simple sentence, resonate, ring like a struck chord.

What would she do if I moved my bishop?

Jude searched for the fly. Dr. Vicki misunderstood. Unsurprising. Turning, she dabbed her nose, and, unable to inhabit the silence, continued.

She smiled. "I'm sorry."

Jude smiled. He felt bad for her. Mary flashed. Jude brushed hair from his brow. Annoyed. Irritated. Let Mary flash brighter. Stronger. Maybe then she would actually do something. Whatever this was? It wasn't this woman's fault.

"I'm not doing so great, am I?" She lifted a pawn, set it back down, and said, "It's your move, if you're ready."

What if the fly had fallen asleep? What would the poor woman prattle on about next? It would be one thing if she was distracting him so that he would, whatever, screw up and lose a bishop. Or a pawn. If she was, playfully, like Father, distracting him to help make him better. At chess. And while Jude forgot the word Father used for … What was that word again? When Father wanted to help me, but pretended that he wasn't? When … oh. Right. Gamesmanship. That was it.

That, and Jude suppressed a smile. That, at least to a degree, was something he could understand as an angle.

But this wasn't that.

So what, then, was it?

With all her talk of school, and fear, Dr. Vicki wasn't trying to create some competitive advantage. And this was a bad thing. Because Jude didn't mind being here. Assuming they could just play chess? It wasn't that bad. He'd even consider coming back. Regularly.

But no.

That was impossible.

Nothing this simple was permissible. It was obvious that, on top of God, and Mother, she liked him. And genuinely. And so, like everyone else—and maybe even more so—she wanted to figure out what was wrong with him.

Only doing that? Figuring out what was wrong? That was impossible. Even if Mother had not selected some person from Our Lady of the Lake. Even if Mother had spent time researching the region for the area's premiere doctor. This was because even Jude didn't know what was wrong. Mary was motivated to help him, but she was also out to hurt Mother. He wasn't dumb. Mary wasn't chess, but she was using Jude, like a pawn. But no matter how hard he tried—the fly, for reasons known only to the fly, buzzed to life, and began crawling up the window—he couldn't see her strategy. Jude saw only what she did. He couldn't predict how she planned to move going forward. Her means to use him. And of course he couldn't share any of this with Rudolph, the Red-Nosed Psychiatrist. Talking about talking to ghosts? Jude didn't need Mary to tell him that if he …

Without thinking Jude moved a knight. Dr. Vicki would have reacted (it wasn't a good move), so he didn't give her a chance. Tired, Jude didn't understand why he was so scared. Why, when at school, there was nothing but fear. Why it was that aside from home—or, strangely, here— fear was something weighing on him, heavy and uncomfortable as a lead apron.

Clouds covered the sun and the room darkened before quickly filling with a different … a false, electric light. The chess pieces cast long shadows, obscuring squares. Dr. Vicki brought a tissue, number four, Jude mindlessly counted, to her nose. Rain fell from the sky, lashed against the glass. Not long before the Freak Accident, Mary and Jude sat behind Mother in the station wagon. They drove through a car wash. Big cloth machines spinning like demented Muppets attacked them, their soap a type of bubbly venom. Mother had laughed. Had smiled. He remembered what she had said about the men, fishing. He wondered if they felt the rain. If they didn't mind getting wet.

"Do you remember your dreams, Jude?"

Not that Jude was going to say anything, but he did, and he didn't. More than anything, he woke up uncomfortable. Disturbed by feeling. Opening his eyes he remained still, aware only of sensation, of dread, of the horrible idea occupying his imagination, the certainty that he was going to do something, that he was going to act in a way that would …

Dr. Vicki continued, speaking slowly, occasionally eyeing him, as if Jude were about to say something and she was prepared to stop, to listen.

"You know something, Jude," she said. "It's perfectly okay, today, to, well, you know, think, 'Who is this lady?' I mean, who am I, anyways? Right?"

She smiled. Brought a tissue to her nose.

"It may not feel this way, but I do understand what you're feeling. Not, say, in terms of what's going on, but when it comes to sitting in some stranger's office, being asked a bunch of questions …"

She trailed off. Tore a tissue into tiny pieces.

"Five," Jude mumbled.

"What," the psychiatrist said. And then, as if making a great life decision, blew her nose. Eyes watering, she sneezed.

"I didn't say anything."

Jude warmed. He willed himself not to blush. To draw attention to himself. Had he just spoken aloud? Mary was always warning him about this.

Dr. Vicki frowned. "You know, I wasn't going to get into this. But your mom. She's worried. She says that she hears you. That you have a habit of talking to yourself. I assured her that it's fine. Normal, even. That she, herself, probably does the same thing more often than …"

Jude ignored the rest of what the doctor said. He resolved to be more careful. While he worried about control, about what he was capable of doing, he knew he wasn't crazy. But he understood what happened when other people thought that you were. And that he couldn't let this happen.

"Jude?"

He looked at the doctor.

"Are you okay?"

He nodded.

"Okay. Well. Fine. Good."

She reached for tissue number six. Jude tried not to smile.

"If you can, though, I think it'd be really great for you to really think about your dreams. What you've been dreaming, how you look at your dreams? This involves noticing how images affect you, how particular images, the things you see, make you feel a certain way. A dream isn't exactly the story you think it is. The dream itself isn't necessarily the "thing"—she made quotes with her fingers—"doing the telling."

Jude didn't have a word for what was wrong with him. But his concern was this: he was going to do something terrible. He did not think he was going to kill someone, like Mother. Unlike Mary, he wasn't angry—he didn't think anyone was particularly awful. But Jude was worried. He knew that he was, in some way, unraveling. That he was not totally in control. While he didn't know the what, he worried about the completed action. How doing something so awful would cost him not so much his life, but whatever value he ascribed to living. He had been feeling this way for a long time now. Since the night of the Freak Accident. So he no longer knew what to think. What anything actually meant.

Dr. Vicki had no way of knowing this. But still—Jude warmed and flushed, and his skin itched—Dr. Vicki thought he was nervous. So long as he didn't say anything, stayed silent and protected his reticence, he had the advantage. But there was nothing easy about any of this. Jude leaned back in his seat. And then, afraid he was being rude, he nodded. He indicated that he understood.

"I know this is complicated," Dr. Vicki said. She smiled. "Dream-tending, which is what I, and what others before me, call this process. Well what you, as dreamer, are asked to do, and I know this sounds weird, is think not so much about what happens during your dream, but to try and forget about your dream as being some sort of story, like a movie."

She paused. Brought the tissue to her nose.

The fly! Where was that fucking fly!

"Instead, ask yourself what would happen if you considered the people, the emotions, the landscapes that are in your dreams separately? What happens if you think of them as being alive, as having their own bodies, their own heartbeats and pulses, and, you know, like you and me, personalities?"

Dr. Vicki tossed her tissue in the trash. She smiled, and, with a flash, bright white as Mary, freed four more from the box.

Seven … Eight … Nine … Ten …

"Well, they become their own animations, their own presences, right? If you look at dreams this way, then, well, dreams become just as alive as you or me. They are important parts of not just us, our natures, but nature itself. Do you see what I mean?"

Dr. Vicki smiled. Had she confused herself? This was possible. Jude certainly didn't understand her rambling, and Jude didn't particularly care. About being here. About any of this. There was nothing this woman, nice as she was— and Jude liked her—could say that would fix him. To Jude, this was obvious. He still cared, generally speaking, but in that way he started caring following Mary's funeral. Which, like a castaway, amounted to a different sort of survival.

He was tired. Of living. Not so much waking up and getting out of bed, but leaving his home? Going to school? Being happy? Or simply not worrying about not doing something hideous? Like walking into a wind gust, existence offered too much resistance. It was impossible, staying on course.

It was possible to imagine giving up. Mary was gone. The world, no matter what happened, would remain forever dark. Stained. Jude was not awaiting an awakening. At any moment the gust was going to turn into a tornado, and he would be blown away.

Bright now, within the darkened room, Mary flickered. White as the psychiatrist's queen. Which, Jude saw, was positioned to attack.

"I feel like I'm confusing you," Dr. Vicki said. "I'm sorry." She smiled. "It's just that sometimes I get so excited. Too excited."

She looked over her shoulder, through Mary, and out the window. The weather was weird. Not sunny or cloudy, wet or dry, the world—like Mary—was a state of suspended animation. The world, more so than usual, did not seem real, was more like a dream.

"Here's the thing, Jude. Dreams are here to help us. Dreams 'live.'"

Again, the thing with her fingers. Making claws of her hands.

"We don't necessarily have dreams, so much as they have us. To make meaning for us. They're a form of medicine. A vaccine that we're born with. Antibodies, in a way." She smiled, pleased with herself. "In that they are a part of us, but apart from us. We come, of course, from nature. Just as much as we come from, say, our parents, our families. Our dreams work to connect everything together. Our dreams restore connections to what's essential, to what's really important. And our dreams help us remember things, as well."

She paused. She touched her nose with a tissue. Smiled. Opened, and then, as if puzzled, closed her mouth. And then, when Jude didn't say anything, she said, "Well for example, then. Do you have, say, a particularly old tree in your yard? A tree that, in its way, is as much a part of your house as your house is, itself?"

Jude didn't know this, but the fly was dead. The fly had fallen to the floor.

Impatient, the psychiatrist continued. She said, "Jude. Honey. What about that big willow tree in your backyard? The one with the swing?"

Before or after the Freak Accident Jude had never seen this woman at his house. Mother must have shown her a picture. That, or Mother had had her over back when he was still in school. One of the things Jude and Mary loved about living on top of the hill was the sense of isolation. That the world around them existed, but that they weren't a part of it. That maybe they, by others, had been put in a sort of childhood quarantine, deemed unsafe to mingle with other people.

Dr. Vicki smiled. "Would you consider that tree part of your house? Like, certainly not a room or anything, but a part of your childhood? Something that, even if it's just maybe, and I know these are some pretty big ideas, but something you might remember when you are older and have moved away? Like away to college. Does that make sense? Or no?"

Jude nodded.

Mary flashed.

"Good," Dr. Vicki said. "So, imagine that you had a dream about that tree. In your dream, and remember, a dream is alive, it is very much a thing, just like you or me, there is a great windstorm. And the tree gets uprooted. Knocked down. Now, I could ask you what you think that means. The tree falling over. But dream-tending. When we take care of our dreams? We go a step further. We think about its—the tree's—sadness. Its pain. We wonder what it thought of its own life. Its own death, even!"

Dr. Vicki smiled. Happy, she used a new tissue.

Eleven, Jude said, inwardly.

She nodded, as if agreeing.

"The dream tender wants to know what the tree is expressing about itself by appearing in his dream. And I know. I can see by the way you're looking at me that you think I'm nuts. That I'm completely bonkers crazy. But this really isn't all that strange! A tree is a living thing, after all. All that you'd do, when tending this dream, is think of it as being just a little bit more alive. Like me." She blew her nose. "Like you."

Whatever her motivations, the psychiatrist had used too many words and distracted herself. Jude willed the fly to move. He could, with a bishop, capture a pawn and control, even if only for two moves—so far as he could see—the center of the board. And if she kept talking? Which, doubtless, she was going to do? While improbable, it was possible that he could gain still more by way of advantage and play the match to, especially given their allotted time (they didn't have all afternoon, Mother was too selfish to spend half a day, parked in a car), a draw. Dr. Vicki looked over her shoulder, smiling, uncertain, confused as to what interested Jude. But the fly was dead. So there would be no moving. There would be no conversation.

Dr. Vicki turned. She faced him. Smiling, she asked about his dream. Directly. He remained silent. Smiling, she said that she'd never force what he said to fit with an explanation or some psychological formula already in existence. When we tend a dream, she continued—Jude half listening, waiting for the fly to move, so he could advance his bishop—images awake, the imagination is animated, and we arrive at a way of being directly connected to Nature. From there, she finished, smiling wider than ever, it's possible to understand not what our dreams mean, but what our dreams are.

The woman, Jude realized, was a swear word away from completely unraveling.

As much as the psychiatrist believed what she was she was blabbering about, Jude wasn't an idiot. Ultimately, she was going to analyze whatever he told her. But this woman was wrong. She misunderstood what caused what was going on. Unless Mary appeared, his situation was hopeless. It was like the fly. Dr. Vicki was aware there was a fly in the room, but she didn't understand what it meant. Jude worried that the fly might have died. That there would be nothing to do if the fly were dead.

Even before the Freak Accident, Jude was accustomed to quiet. Conditioned to comfortably pass through nothingness, with what "others" considered confidence, "others"—most notably Mother's friends, which amounted to anyone from Our Lady of the Lake— weren't. These were people ill-equipped to occupy silence. These were people who felt that if someone wasn't speaking, something was wrong. Worse, these were people who felt that if they had a thought the idea remained incomplete until voiced. Until what they were thinking was spoken.

And what people thought?

This was even worse.

Here, there was no how. Most thoughts were ignored, or unrealized, with considered thoughts not so much creations, or even actions, but things arriving with the gravity of lightning strikes, charges not so much positive or negative as fleeting – sparks, really – proof only of the existence of excess, with this (the glut) spilling from open mouths masked as thought, defined as dialogue, but nothing that could ever pass for ideas.

So Jude wasn't surprised when Dr. Vicki cracked.

When, smiling, she told him that, at some point, he simply had to talk. That he was going to have to tell her about his dream, and that if he didn't …

Here she cut off.

Left the rest of her thought to gleam, to sparkle sharp as a threat.

And then, as if realizing her mistake, she said, her tone assuming the form of an apology, "Maybe you just don't understand. Or maybe I am just too confusing, and that's why you aren't speaking!"

Like most adults, Dr. Vicki had no clue how to speak to children. Of course she was confusing. He knew most of the words she used. He could even string most of their meanings together. But there was more to a conversation than speaking. Than words. Like it was with most adults, remembering or forgetting? It didn't matter. Jude had no idea what she was saying.

He did get why, though.

And so he felt even worse for her.

Only there was nothing he could say that would not alarm her. Given all her talk of tending, of thinking of dreams as, well, whatever. Breathing? This woman, well, if she heard what Jude had to say, she would be horrified. Alive or dead, animate or otherwise, she would think of both Jude and his dream as something invented. As zombie sorts of Frankensteins. A draft passed through the room and Dr. Vicki adjusted her coat. She reached for a tissue—number twelve, if Jude had counted correctly—and dabbed her nose.

Not that this mattered. Mary knew her brother. That he was gentle. And how, even though he had no reason to, he displayed kindness. So she had prepared for this eventuality. They had even practiced, rehearsed what Jude was going to say. Mary didn't know about the fly, but this didn't matter. This psychiatrist, given that she was Mother's friend, was unpredictable by default. This psychiatrist, given that she was a psychopath? Well, she had to stop talking before something (Mary wasn't sure what) terrible happened. And the only way for that to happen was for Jude to say something. It was necessary to control the message.

"Tell her," Mary said.

Jude closed his eyes. Opened them. He thought it a natural response, and didn't want to look in Mary's direction. What Jude wanted, though? He wanted to tell Dr. Vicki. Not the story Mary had created—she flashed, and Jude ignored her—but one of his real, actual dreams. Or at least what it was like, waking up. How his shoulders and knees were so numb, how his bones ached (as if pins and needles had stuck him in place) and he couldn't move. How his chest didn't hurt, exactly, but that the pressure suggested it was about to. That he wasn't sure where he was, or, worse, that he was somewhere terrible, like jail, because of something horrible he had done. He wanted help. Relief.

He said, "I'm sorry. I don't mean to be rude."

Dr. Vicki, as if bitten by a spider, straightened. She smiled. Reaching across the table, she squeezed Jude's hand. No doubt leaning on something she had learned in school, she, too, closed her eyes, and then opened them.

"Jude, honey," she said. She let go of his hand and leaned back in her seat. She knocked over one of her knights. "Believe me, I get it. I understand. This may seem strange, but I see a psychiatrist, too. Living is not easy. If it was—"

She cut off, only not as sharply. She reached for a tissue and dabbed her nose.

"Well let's just say that living isn't easy, and leave it at that. Did you want to tell me about your dream? About one of your dreams?"

Thirteen, Jude thought. He wondered who would win. Dr. Vicki, with her tissues. Or Father, when it came to clearing his throat. He remembered that morning, after church. How his nose was bleeding and Mother was crying and all Father did was drive. Drive and clear his throat.

"I'm not sure I know how," Jude said.

Mary flashed.

This line? This was not part of the script. None of this would be any good if Dr. Vicki suspected that Jude was lying. But Jude wasn't an actor. He was human. He had been distracted.

"It's a weird thing, isn't it?" Dr. Vicki said. "Dreams are such bizarre things! Don't …" She crumpled her tissue, and tossed it in the trash. "In a way, I don't even want you to think. At least about telling me a story. Don't even try. Just try to remember what you can remember, and the rest will work itself out perfectly. I promise. Remember all that talk about images? That's what I was talking about. Think about those. About them. And the rest will sort itself out. Sound okay?"

Jude said that it did.

"Okay then," she said. "Where would you like to begin?"

Before Jude could speak, Mary started talking.

And what she said, Jude repeated. He followed her pauses, her calls for inflection. And when it was over, five, or ten minutes later, he could have cried – although he didn't know why.

And Dr. Vicki grabbed herself a tissue.

Fourteen.

APRIL 11 – 25, 1983

Jude, following every snack, meal, and glass, box, or pouch of juice, made himself puke. This had been happening since Lent. Eventually, there was nothing Mother could do. She kept him home from school.

Because he did not have a temperature, and because he did not present anything other by way of symptoms, Dr. Greene, given that Jude had been seen by, and was awaiting word from a series of specialists, said there was no reason why Jude couldn't, so long as he believed he was up for it, accompany Mother to Our Lady of the Lake, thus enabling her to work.

Mother believed that Jude was up for it.

Jude didn't hate the Church. Before the Freak Accident, Church was like a calendar that consulted him. While most of the other boys his age used sports to mark the changing seasons, Jude loved Advent, Lent, Easter, and Christmas, even finding in Passover and the Holy Days of Obligation (especially Pentecost and All Saints Day) something to wake him from his day-to-day reverie. Thanks to Mother and Mrs. Kruty, the Sundays before and during these occasions looked special. Our Lady of the Lake's interior transformed, upon and around the altar extra candles and flowers bright like strung Christmas lights—while from the ceiling and around stone statues huge wreaths and great swathes of thick fabric glittered like carved pumpkins. Even the stories Father Hours read were more interesting. Jesus, when bothered, became exciting.

Supposedly, you couldn't have good without evil. Jude wasn't sure about that, but it was true that part of the reason Church became, if not fun, well certainly less boring, was because summers were so long, and, when it came to God, and Jesus, not much happened after Easter and before Halloween. During July and August—and even into the fall—Father Hours, after vaguely referencing one of the readings, used the pulpit to prattle off a series of contradictions that carried as much verbal currency as a high school carwash. Our Lady of the Lake's interior smoking hot, eyes bright and open, Jude, as if feverish, his hair damp with sweat, dreamed.

The idea that nothing came from nothing had to be impossible, and while Jude didn't believe in God, at least not like his parents, he didn't not believe in God, like Mary. None of it made sense. Why was this so difficult to admit? To hear one person say one thing, and for them to say it like only they were right? Well, this made everyone— because everyone spoke this way—sound just as wrong, or as far removed from what was "right," as the other person.

Jude didn't particularly like Father Hours. The man was like a vegetable. A cabbage. Something his mom insisted was good for him. More importantly, though, Jude did not dislike priests, generally. In fact, the opposite held true. How these men gave over the entirety of their lives to the idea of something? Even someone boring, like Father Hours? This was amazing. Because priests certainly weren't right. At least not necessarily. Even if God was (and Jude, gun to head, would have said yes, before no), well, there was just no way to know.

After all, who had made Him?

And then who, or what, had made the who (or the what) that had made God?

Maddening.

The idea was just too crazy—but in a good, dazzling, way. And so this is how Jude spent homilies: pleasantly lost in thought, almost dizzy, de-creating everything that everyone had to say.

Before the Freak Accident, Jude had no interest in dying. He wanted to be alive, always. That's how much he enjoyed living. But when bored, say, during church—especially when forced to endure some marathon like Palm Sunday, or when someone was baptizing their baby—he did think that at least one cool thing about dying would be that he would finally find out something.

Now, though. With Mary being dead, and unwilling to talk about anything other than Mother? Refusing to answer anything that actually mattered? Well, everything, on top of being terrible, was more confusing. This, while new, was not normal. Living certainly didn't seem as important, and even less so, if you were unhappy.

Back when Mother told him what, so long as he wasn't going to school, he'd be doing instead, Jude argued that he was old enough to stay home, alone. He even pushed, insisting that, when at Our Lady of the Lake, there was nothing to do, and that there was no way she could argue his point because this point was, as a matter of fact, true. Mother would never agree, but who cared? Mary said that did not matter, insisting he speak up—and repeatedly—because that him offering resistance was something Mother would expect him to do. Jude shrugged. Ambivalent, it would have been cool staying home. But he didn't mind accompanying Mother to work, either. Alone, or at church, how else would he occupy his time, Monday through Friday, nine until two?

Unlike Sundays, he dressed comfortably, and Mother, busy with whatever, left him in the nursery. In addition to homework (Mother visited his school's office every Friday afternoon, picking up the week's missed work), Jude brought books—Thursdays, they stopped at the library before heading home—and his art supplies. This was peaceful, easy, living. After the first week, Mother, on the condition that he promised never to enter those areas of the church strictly prohibited to all lay parishioners (this, of course, included the church's tower), encouraged Jude to stretch his legs, going so far as to grant him permission to go outside. The only stipulation? He must promise to never cross the street.

"If you want to visit the lake," Mother said, pointing in the direction of the water. "Or walk around the park? Well, Father Hours and I think that would be just great! And I'll arrange for it. We just need you to be patient. That street … well, you know how busy it is. And there's no crosswalk. Mrs. Kruty, myself, even Father Hours would be happy to accompany you. I know it doesn't seem like much …" She raised a hand, whirled it above her head. "But there's a lot going on around here. So just find one of us and ask, honey. Okay? We'll find the time, no problem. Sound good?"

Mary nodded. Jude looked on, motionless. It blew his mind. How no one knew that he just didn't care.

Other than a few Mary-driven trips to the tower, Jude didn't go anywhere. And, given that these visits were clandestine, usually when Mother was away from the building, running some unnecessary errand, the adults (Mother, Father Hours, and Mrs. Kruty) worried. When at Our Lady of the Lake Jude did not eat or drink, so no one heard him vomiting. If anyone took to spying, they would see him carrying on strange, near cryptic conversations with himself. But, so far as he knew, they didn't. Given that talking with Mary left him sated, and, often, animated, his cheeks flushed, and his eyes bright, he looked healthy, almost happy. Certainly nothing looked the matter. This left only his isolation and his reticence, for others to consider, a problem in need of fixing. Mother declared Father Hours' decision to escort Jude to the tower wonderful, so long as Jude wasn't too uncomfortable, given his fear of heights.

Mary, ever-present, had processed the information. Jude was afraid of heights, and Mother knew this? Jude could not be sure, but it was possible Mary was surprised Mother knew something that she didn't. There was no point in asking her, or wasting time trying to figure it out. Mary, as if she were fictitious, a character from Wonderland, answered questions with riddles. And her expression was as expansive as a mannequin's.

"All the more reason, then," Father Hours said, smiling. "Might bring about a bit of confidence. Fear not," the priest said. "That's the most common phrase found in the Bible, you know."

Confused, Helen smiled, blithely.

Mrs. Kruty agreed, wholeheartedly. And then she wondered—aloud—if she should pack the boys a lunch.

Mary stared.

Mother frowned.

Father Hours looked around.

Jude nodded.

Father Hours stood behind Jude, halved by the stairwell's sheer angle, his bald spot bright. Mary, worried Jude would somehow let on that he had been to the tower before, coached him. She told him when to stop, when to grab the railing, and when to look up. She told him when to resume walking. He was, after all, afraid of heights.

Her plan was working, but, irritated, Jude didn't think people, especially people like Father Hours and Mrs. Kruty, paid attention the way Mary did. They cared, but it was because of this concentrated attention that they were blind to other facets of Jude's existence. He didn't listen to everything Mary had to say. When worried Jude didn't seem concerned enough, Mary disappeared, and then, with a pop!, appeared in front of him, an action meant to slow him down, or block his way. Instinctively, Jude, startled, stopped. This, to the priest, presented the illusion of fear. Of nerves. Father Hours, breathing heavily, heart thumping, told Jude to take his time, that he was doing just fine.

Jude had to be able to walk through Mary. She was real—but in the way steam was real. What, aside from his own uncertainty, would stop him? Doubt was a real problem, though, and difficult to overcome. It was like the men on Ripley's Believe It Or Not! who broke cinder blocks with their hands, or who chewed and swallowed glass. If they doubted, they would seriously injure themselves—or, worse, die. What if now, when talking about Mary, the opposite was true? Not that any of that really mattered. In truth, the thought of walking through his sister was troubling. Almost disgusting. More than that, though … what if passing through his sister threw off whatever sort of earthly balance, or buoyancy, she maintained? Jude wasn't willing to risk ruining her.

"Remember, Jude," Mary said. "Mother told him you are afraid of heights."

What was Jude supposed to say?

"Nothing," Mary said, reading his mind. She blinked, as if working to make sure Jude caught her eye. "You are acting too confidently. You cannot move as though you are not afraid. Remember how scared you were the first time we came up here? Father Hours is going—"

"Well I, for one, am impressed," Father Hours said.

Breathing heavily, the shoulders of his black shirt shiny and made, with sweat, a bright sort of black, his glasses had fogged over, but he was too tired to clear them. "I thought you were supposed to be afraid of heights! But you're more like a cat than a ..." Coughing, and wheezing, he managed, "I'd like to say it's the dust. Or allergies." The priest smiled. He laughed and rubbed his belly. "Just give me a minute. But this is good. Take a look out the window. Consider the view. And then I can show you even more than I intended to, given how comfortable you seem."

Mary flashed.

Jude nodded ... indicated it was okay.

A beautiful afternoon, Cascadilla Lake disappeared into the distance, a plane of water wrinkled, like a crumpled sheet of paper pulled from the trash and smoothed over. Since Jude began accompanying mother to work the weather had been lousy, cold and rainy, overcast and dreary, never warm, the sort of days that perfectly suited Jude's mindset and mood. That today, a Tuesday, the sun seemed, of its own accord, to have risen early, giving way to a vast sky pale and bright, an especially oxygenated sort of blue, was surprising. Elmira's scalloped West Hill in panoramic vista, its trees full of leaves laser-beam green, tall pines, dark and rich in their clusters, rose as if purposefully planted there. Warm and lacking humidity, the air a lovely medium and still as a painting (except for far out over the water where passing breezes built and collapsed many waves), insects, confused as to whether it was summer or spring, buzzed about curiously, idiotically, smacking into buildings and trees.

Far out, where the lake met the sky, the hillside was less green, soft, like chalk, the impression of the horizon wavelike, the image of a frequency rising and falling. Overhead cloud cover undulating, a canopy rich with definition and varying degrees of darkness, the sky set apart like crenellations formed by the presence of one another. And between breaks in the clouds the sky blue sky.

The sun, high overhead, was bright as a star. There was so much light. So much so that every person and structure and angle and feature accented by this warm late-day sun was improved, every boy and girl and tree in the park was softened and refined and not so much colored by beauty but as if presenting itself in a shimmering sort of outline, readying itself for discovery. Even shadows were seemingly distressed, unsure as if, recently cast, they should submit to their sources. Sounds were certainly being made, but, up in the tower, there was nothing but silence. The phenomenon was strange. Like looking at Father's screen saver and waiting for the object—some digital box or ball—to meet with one of the computer's four corners.

"Amazing, isn't it?" Father Hours said. He lifted a foot, as if to make for the window, then thought better of it. He would wait another few minutes.

Jude nodded. The other evening—Mother had to work late—Mary had insisted that they visit the tower. The sun had almost completed its arc, the sun had set below the hillside, and color spread across the horizon. Like a flame alighting a bed of coals, the hillside in outline. Electric blue. Deep purple and pink. And this color fading, the sky assuming, like grains of sand in some mystic mandala, shades orange and yellow and turquoise green before yielding to evening's celestial blue, distant stars poking through this ancient atmosphere, bright as stars. She had led him through the stone chamber, deeper, towards the clock (what Jude considered the back of the church), much further than they had ever ventured before.

"Sorry," Father Hours said.

Jude shrugged.

"Quite the view, though, no?"

Jude nodded. It was.

"If you look out far enough, there, to your left, if you follow the west side of the lake, look back into the hillside a bit, you'll see what looks like a long, light-green, line. That's a shadow, actually. That's the road that leads to your home."

The Bendzes lived in the middle of nowhere, and Jude was skeptical. The land around his home, its tall green grasses an invitation to giant grasshoppers and well-fed groundhogs, was parceled into great pastures perfectly symmetrical, a patchwork as presented from an airplane. Come fall—Jude's favorite season—these grasses were cut and rolled into huge, round hay bales, in appearance commodities not so much collected, but, like art, objects as if arranged for some specific aesthetic or reason, a code which Jude could not decipher.

Jude looked through the window, out and over the lake. Huh. The priest was right. Set within the hillside a green line snaked up and across the forest. This was a path that Jude had driven so often it was easy, from high atop the tower, to picture.

The very top of the hill ran straight for miles, rising and falling, rising and falling, before, like a rollercoaster, dropping down West Hill, Mother's least favorite part of the drive. Long gravel driveways led to late-model doublewides surrounded by tightly moved lawns pocked yellow with dandelions. Yellow daffodils made the green grass greener, and green grass made the yellow flowers brighter. A gentle give and take. More proof, Mother pointed out, that God is great.

From inside the tower the hilltop was not so much a direction, but a destination. All of Endwell presented before them, it was simple to determine north from south, east from west. Jude enjoyed the drive, and, when the weather allowed, would roll down his window, a means, since Mary's death, to prevent Mother from speaking. The stink of the cultivated country fields, farmland ripe with manure and fish oil, intensified as Mother built speed, and was often strong enough to shut her up completely.

And how, too, through Jude's window, Cascadilla Lake. Dreaming, Jude pictured the lake breaking and spilling from its southern shore to slam Endwell, devouring first the waterfront district with its public golf course and pretentious farmers market before rising to overtake those rundown apartments dotting the grid of streets surrounding The Commons, tenants and landlords alike scrambling for safety and clinging to the shingles of steepled rooftops only to be lifted by the rapidly rising current like so many leaves in the gutter, the women and the men kicking and screaming, the water cresting below second story windows. And how, through the windows, moms with their bright-eyed babies hanging low on their hips looked out onto the hopelessness, this sea of swirling mud-brown water submerging all of Endwell proper and drowning every dog and cat, every man, woman, and baby. Not even Our Lady of the Lake saved.

"Penny for your thoughts," Father Hours said. He took the remaining steps and managed to squeeze behind Jude. Breathing heavily, he leaned against the wall and considered what constituted his view. Mary had disappeared.

Mother hated Jude's favorite part of the drive. How the road rose, crested, and then fell. Streaming through the window the potent rise of dirt and pine, that mixture of life and decay stemming from what remained of Endwell's old growth forest. Nearby, countless tree trunks. Down the hill, in the near distance, the tops of very tall trees. Here the passage was steep, and Mother all but braked to a complete stop. Mumbling, she steered through switchbacks and hairpin bends, her brake lights bleeding to bloody the shadows a rich, ruby red. Before them her headlights illuminating silver guardrails and behind those rocky till and sheer moraine walls rich with fossils from some long-ago world rising into a place populated by varying degrees of darkness, this world where field and furrow gave way to rocky escarpments before, eventually, just the ringing silence of the silent, watchful, trees.

Jude shrugged. And then, unsure if that was the proper response, he nodded.

The priest cast a shadow, making the window a mirror. Gone was West Hill and Cascadilla Lake, and there, like a view, were Jude's features, his face. No one thought that he resembled Mary. Everyone was pretty much right. Except for their eyes. Because Jude's were brown, people failed to notice that, in size and shape, the similarities between Jude and his sister were unmistakable. These were the moments, the small, sudden reminders when it was impossible, even if she was right there, white and glowing, not to miss her.

"I don't mean to pry," Father Hours said. Atop the steps he had calmed. His breathing had settled. "And I don't even really expect you to answer, if we're being honest, here. But"—the priest brought a hand to the side of his face—"well, it strikes me as unfair that no one asks you about Mary. About Mary being dead, I mean to say. Not to put things too bluntly—"

He broke off and began coughing. But not like Father. He sounded more like one of the old people, from the hospital. It wasn't hot, but the priest was sweating. His round face was very red. Smiling, he looked around the space. But there was nothing to see. As if making a tough decision he nodded, and continued, speaking with more force than necessary.

"Well, sometimes there is a time and a place. There is no vaccine for these lives we live, you know. There is no inoculation that will ward off feeling." He sighed. "I like to think religion inoculates, that it's a sort of immunization, but it's not, really. I know better than to believe in something as magical as that."

From him the feeling that he was going to say more, that he wasn't done, but was unsure how to continue. And then, "A situation like this. Well, I'll be honest with you, Jude. It seems like I go to, or prepare for, in some way, a funeral a day. Every day I drive out to meet someone who has lost a brother. Or a wife of forty years. At least that's the way it feels. The way it seems. It's why they pay me the big bucks." He smiled.

Father Hours was, in many respects, proud. Confident. Jude knew that Mary saw only "priest." Adult. Given that her youth and her pride represented her particular brand of childhood, adults—especially those in positions of authority, like priests—were certain sorts of enemies. Here, more so than ever before, stood a man. A guy. Every Sunday he got up in front of one hundred people and spoke as if God told him what to say. Or that he understood what Jesus had been saying thousands of years ago. And that was dumb. Even Jude knew—there were a few honest teachers at Our Lady of the Lake, Boys—that the people, thousands of years ago, understood that what people like Mark wrote wasn't meant to be taken literally. Obviously these writers wanted to be taken seriously— why else write?—but, like Aesop, they were writing stories, and not even so much that, which was to say tales meant to teach something, but more like commercials. Latter-day advertisements. Like so many priests, he was terrible with children. When with Father Hours, or when listening to him talk, Jude worked through what it meant to respect someone while not particularly liking them—or, like Mother, feeling an obligation to love them.

"Anyways," he said, scratching the back of his neck. "Everyone wants to know how you're doing. How you're feeling. And that's fine. That's normal. Your parents have been through a lot. And they're still going through a lot. They've, as you know, changed. And they're never coming back. The only reason I say that is because I think you know this." He covered his mouth with his hand. Spoke softer.

"I think you're mature enough to handle some things other kids can't. Or wouldn't be able to. But what I don't think they, your parents, and your teachers, what I don't think they understand is how much you've changed. And that no matter how much they might want to protect you, or for you to be the same, it's impossible. You're never coming back, either. There isn't going to be some breakthrough. There's no cure for grief. Especially not when concerning a loss of this magnitude. And that's okay. And it's okay, in a way, for your parents not to understand this. It's O … K! That's the important part of what I'm trying to say. There's no right or wrong here. These are unchartered waters. These really and truly are …" And the priest cleared his throat. "Trying times."

Father Hours pressed a hand against the wall. Head backed against the wood, he looked up. Jude had stood in that spot. Had seen what there was to see. With a pop! Mary materialized next to the priest. It was strange, how she cast no light. How she just was. As bright and as white as a single cloud in a crazy blue sky. It was incredible, how she seemed contained. That she made everything around her darker.

Jude looked through the window. Jude looked through his reflection and studied that place where, on the West Hill, the road cut across the earth. Jude could place himself inside Mother's station wagon, her face panic-stricken, a line of cars behind them. Before them the huge houses dotting the lakefront, and then the smaller cottages, the summer rentals like fans at a concert jammed together shoulder to shoulder, or one of those multi-colored strings of flags associated with some other's religion. And then the sun-bled asphalt through the windshield splashed with shadows bending from the trees making everything difficult to see, like staring through shutters rapidly opening and closing before, like that, they were out; there were no more trees; there was no more shadow … just light. The road level, through Mothers' window the lake's great lapping water separated from the road by a wide swathe of regularly mowed lawn, a guardrail running its wide sweeping arc—

"You're frightened, Jude, aren't you?"

Mary flashed.

Jude rested his head against the glass. He was tired.

"You're worried about Mary. You're scared about what's happened to her."

The priest was, in part, correct.

"Jude," Mary said. "I'm fine. You have no reason to worry. I will not lie to you. Him? Father Hours? Other than boring, and out of shape—"

Jude turned, considered Mary. Was she making a joke?

Father Hours believed he had captured Jude's attention. Surprised—he had been ready to drop the conversation— he opened his mouth to speak.

"Jude," Mary said. "Father Hours. Mother. They are ready to tell you all about God. About this great big ghost in the sky. But what would they say if you told them, if you told Father Hours that I am not gone, that I am more visible than God, and that he could see me if he just believed, that I am standing right here, right here on the top of his church right next to him, carrying on a conversation with you, Mother's son, and that I have more to say than anyone?"

"Jude," Father Hours said. "It's perfectly reasonable for you to fear for Mary. To more than miss her. And don't worry." He smiled. "I'm not going to get all religious on you. But I do hope you'll hear me out. At least for a minute."

Jude nodded.

"I am not here to tell you that Father Hours is mean, Jude. I am not going to say much, really, considering that I do not know the man, personally."

There was a sailboat on the lake. It was moving, from west to east—and quickly—but, from where Jude stood, the object looked as motionless as dried paint on canvas.

"God," Father Hours said. "And this is where it gets confusing. I certainly don't mean to speak ill of anyone. And I'm not. Not genuinely. Women like Mrs. Kruty, for instance. Or Mrs. Cooney, your teacher. Or any of the others who help with Sunday School. They provide an invaluable service. It's important, and I really believe this, for children, for all of us, from the moment we are born, to be in touch with God. But you poor kids. You poor kids …

"What you're taught when you're little? Young? While the intent behind the message is wonderful, even good, the stories, the way that the Word is delivered? Well, honestly?" He removed his hand, and then re-covered his mouth. "Well, plain and simple, that's just no good. Because God. It's not like life can be marked off in years. Well, you see, when—"

This is what interested Jude: how many words a person spoke. How it was, in fact, possible, to know, exactly, how many words a person had spoken while alive – but that no one did. That no one had ever set up such an experiment. Meanwhile—he had seen a sanitized version of this particular horror on Ripley's Believe It Or Not!—horrible hypotheses had been carried out. In the thirteenth century, King Frederick II of Germany wanted to know what language children would speak if they were never exposed to language. He assigned foster mothers to care for fifty babies. The women, undoubtedly peasants; poor to be sure, but certainly persons capable of love; people who were, themselves, loved by God … well, they were told to bathe and nurse the babies, to keep the children nourished and clean, but they were forbidden—and this by a punishment equal to, if not worse than death—to fondle, cuddle, or, obviously, talk when they were in the presence of the babies.

What language did the babies speak? the voiceover had teased before the commercial break.

Jude's guess was German.

The correct answer?

They didn't. The experiment failed. (Of succeeded.) Every child died. Turns out people need, just as much as anything, human contact, a connection, the warmth that arises from other sentient beings … Even if it's just hearing them talking.

Jude had believed it.

"Jude," Mary said. "Trust me. Father Hours is not a bad man, but it is not good of him to confuse you. Suppose I was unable to come back. Imagine if I was not here. Would talking about me, to him, amount to anything? You'd still know what had happened, and your life would be even worse than it is now. Mother is a lie, and only you know the truth. And yes. She is suffering. He is right about that. But what she feels, now, is a splinter. It is—"

"What I'm trying to say is this," Father Hours said. Unaware he competed to hold Jude's attention, the priest straightened, proud he commanded the boy's interest. "A long time ago, people were writing about Jesus. About the great things he did. More importantly, at least in my opinion, they recorded the many great things he said. His way of life. His approach to living."

A pause. Jude wondered who would race to fill it.

It was the priest.

He looked at Mary. She stared, blankly.

"Paul was the first. The first to write, I mean. You've heard about him, I'm sure, but not like this. Then comes Mark. Now, remember, this is years, this is decades after Jesus was crucified. I'm sure you talk about the oral tradition at school? When talking about the Indians? Well, the same thing was going on back then. People met and they talked about Jesus. And so when men like Mark, or whomever, wrote about Jesus, they weren't trying to get down everything. They weren't writing like people do today. He didn't care when Jesus was born. He didn't care about dates. And see, Jude, the people back then who read Mark? And then Matthew, John, and Luke, or what we priests call Luke Acts? They knew that they were reading stories. Unlike your mo—"

Father Hours affected a cough.

Like Father, he cleared his throat.

"Unlike really good people, like Mrs. Kruty, they didn't necessarily take these stories literally. They read them, and they shared them with their friends, with those who would listen, like lessons. Like, and forgive me if I already mentioned this, Aesop's fables."

Mary was not talking. Incredible. It was obvious Father Hours was talking about Mother – and that he wasn't being kind, either.

Was it possible that Mary was listening?

No chance, had Mary been alive. She didn't believe adults were idiots. Mary just considered adults smart about dumb things.

Being dead, however?

Who knew?

What Mary did, and why, was just as mysterious as her existing. For whatever reason, it seemed like she wanted him listening.

Father Hours assumed he was getting somewhere, and the priest pushed on. Mary stared. Jude felt anxious. Concerned. Worried. Something was bound to come from this.

"Speaking of Indians," Father Hours said. "They have the most wonderful saying. Like one of our Gospels, I couldn't tell you who, exactly, said it. And, if you ask me, we, as in us adults, we theologians, should spend a lot more time studying Indians. The Native Americans, I should say. Anyways"—he coughed—"excuse me." And he waved his hand in front of his face. "Must be something in the air."

Had he hit, and passed through Mary? Jude thought so, but he couldn't be sure. He wished he had been paying closer attention. Mary remained motionless. She did nothing.

He breathed heavily. Said, "Anyways, unlike us, unlike our parents and teachers who complain and say, 'Don't just sit there, do something,' what they, what the Indians say to their kids is, 'Don't just do something, sit there.'"

The priest paused for effect. Or because he was out of breath. Of course Jude couldn't be sure, but it seemed like Mary was interested. If she wanted him to do something, she wouldn't be standing there, silent.

"See, they, the Indians, well the thing is, and I happen to agree with this, well it's that they, their Elders, well they think a true sign of wisdom is sitting, and seeing, when there is nothing to see. And then, along those lines, sitting, and listening, when there is nothing to hear.

"We have people like that in our faith, Jude. They're called mystics. Surely you've heard of Joan of Arc? St. Francis of Assisi? Anyways, and I suppose the reason I'm saying all this is because, not to sound weird, or creepy, but I do sit, and I do watch you, Jude. And you seem cut from the same cloth. I'm not saying you're a mystic. I'm not saying you're going to grow up and become a priest. Who knows what you'll become! But what I am saying in this long-winded, roundabout way of mine is that there are a couple of ways to take the Bible, that there are basically two ways to process all the stuff we priests, and your teachers, talk about. There's literally, meaning that you literally believe Noah built an Ark and captured two of every animal that was living at the time. Or Seriously. You understand the Bible is a tool, one of many, by which people can live. And you …"

Father Hours coughed, his face bright red, and becoming redder …

"You, and I've no doubt of this, are the sort of person who takes the Bible seriously. Assuming …" The priest smiled. "Well, assuming you consider any of this at all. Do you know what word is used in the New Testament, more than any other?"

Jude looked at Mary. If she knew, she was not saying. Jude was no longer worried. Now he was just confused. He felt like this was an important moment. That something significant was happening. He wanted to speak. He was surprised when Mary nodded.

"Love?"

Father Hours seemed surprised. Mary seemed to move closer. Jude was certain he heard a sound. Even Father Hours turned, and looked in her direction. "That's nice, Jude," he said. Turning. "That's a very nice answer. But that was sort of a trick question. The word is 'altar.' It's mentioned twenty-three times. Know how I remember that?"

Jude didn't.

"Have you heard of Michael Jordan, yet?"

Jude hadn't.

"You will. He's a basketball player. One of my guilty pleasures? Watching basketball. Anyways, that's his number. Twenty-three. I use it when I can as a mnemonic device. A way to remember things."

Mary was glowing. Jude didn't know what she … he didn't know what any of this meant.

"But that's only part of the story, right? The New Testament, I mean. That's only half. That's not taking the Old Testament into account. When we do that, your answer is much closer. Want to take another guess?"

Mary shook her head. No.

"No? Well, it's actually not a word. That would be Lord, or something like that. I meant phrase. The most common phrase is 'Be not afraid'. And I suppose that's what I've been getting at, Jude. Don't be afraid to do what you think is right. Don't …"

The priest stopped talking. The tower was dark, cool, and quiet. There were no cobwebs, and there was no dust. Maybe Mrs. Kruty cleaned the place? Probably. Jude had visited the tower just last week, and the area looked the same. Visited, yes—books had been moved, candles removed—but otherwise untouched. It was impossible to remember what Mary had been talking about, generally. Specifically, though, that was easy. Mary had been talking about Mother. She spoke of nothing else. Cold air drafted across the space, as if making for the staircase.

Mary moved behind the priest. That spot she once inhabited black, as dark as anything Jude had ever seen. Jude knew that Father Hours could not see Mary. He did not think that Jude was following Mary, but detected movement … again, like everyone, he misunderstood. He believed Jude was interested in what he had to say. Jude did not understand what Mary was doing. Jude knew that, like everyone, the priest was accustomed to Jude's silence. Jude also knew that Father Hours was, nonetheless, disappointed. Actions were one thing. But silence. To not speak one single word? He knew the boy was quiet. Had heard he refused to speak with his psychiatrist. Mary said that Father Hours was slow to consider Jude a fake, but that he didn't think he was sick, either.

Jude grabbed the railing and looked down. Unlike before, there was nothing to see. There was nothing to feel. This part of Our Lady of The Lake offered security. He was safe. From the other end of the building the cathedral's bells called the top of the hour. He had not been paying attention, so could not remember which. Maybe noon? Had the bells been ringing for a long time? Jude raised his head and closed his eyes. He made fists of his hands. Like the tower, Jude was compressed, completely still.

He didn't know what to say. But he knew what he had to do. It was time to not just watch and listen. He needed to take Mary seriously.

Mary nodded.

Jude stared.

December 26, 1982, and Points Soon After

Mary was smart. Jude was, too. While the siblings read widely, they favored speculative fiction. That which was presented in abstract seemed, to them, especially true. The popularity of a book-made-movie (the story's protagonist, pitted against a dead civilization, armed with only her wits and a simple weapon) led to the creation, and mass production, of toys like AimZing, a realistic set of bow and arrows, advertised as safe for children.

Their parents had been divided. Mom (who prohibited games like Jarts) wasn't okay with the toy. Dad didn't mind. By this point the couple had been for so long agreeing that disagreements rarely amounted to much of anything, as neither knew how to properly form their position without fear of hurting the others' feelings. When faced with dispute, both were so quick to acquiesce that one point bled into another, and logic, rendered circular, was pointless, no longer meaningful. Because Mary and Jude pressed the issue, Helen and James discussed, rather than debated the issue, after dinner and before bed, somewhat casually, if not absently, working less to carry the day than ensuring they did not wound the other.

If asked, neither could say, with certainty, who allowed the toy to enter their home. Neither understood how the other had arrived at a decision. This was one of a few ways the couple expressed love. Quietly. One. To the other. Often saying little, to nothing, at all. When Mary died, this did not change.

Regarding the Freak Accident, Endwell did not know what happened. All anyone knew was that a little girl died. To the extent Endwell understood anything, they only wondered: How could this be? And to the degree they assigned blame, they worried. What sort of parents would create a climate where children inhabit so wide a space that such violence, however accidental, has the room to take place? They didn't need to know everything. But they would not allow confusion to override understanding.

Naturally, this sort of truth does not exist. Mother. And Mary. They might as well have been alone. And so after reading the story running beneath the headline above the fold (FREAK ACCIDENT KILLS LOCAL STUDENT), Endwell's collected questions remained. They became, in the absence of proof, a lesser form of truth, one tier below answers ...

Ideas.

Speculation.

This is what they learned: The rumor that the boy had killed his sister? That the siblings, armed with their toy bow and their toy arrow, were playing a sort of William Tell? This is something that, days later, would be deemed a lie. Untrue. There had been an investigation, though. After police arrived on the scene, the EPD, in service of its citizenry, offered two detectives. As far as the people knew, that is where inquiry both began, and ended. What, Endwell asked, about a social worker? Or: What of family? Friends? How about family friends? Endwell—even after all that would later happen—remained unsure. Nothing became, even among people in positions of authority, popular opinion. Of course the detectives were suspicious.

Of course every record was examined. Every stone was turned. But because there was never an arrest, let alone a trial, there could never be conviction.

There was conjecture. Questions leading to more questions. These, in the absence of answers, lead to the wobbly, the uncertain theory that sure, maybe the death hadn't been intentional, but this wasn't the same as saying it had been accidental. I mean, Endwell mused, just look at what happened to Mary. Consider what happened to Jude.

Nothing forgotten, the circumstances surrounding what happened certainly were strange. Why was the girl outside? And when it came to her brother … Or, perhaps more interestingly—if not more importantly—what sort of mother created a space wherein—

Oh, wait, Endwell thought, We've already been over that.

It was along this line of thinking that sympathy yielded to suspicion.

There were many inconsistencies. At first—following the flashing lights and phone calls, coupled with the chaotic Endwell innuendo—information spread.

Through Endwell.

A small, cloistered community.

A city where people first took pride on being, and then on being from Endwell, news of the Freak Accident, like a great fire, spread from home to home. The fire roared, and rumors, as if thrust by great wind gusts, leapt from West Hill to find fuel within city blocks, alighting upon the rooftops of distant neighborhoods. Parents inured with their own hardships welcomed the distraction and called one another at first timidly, warily, almost with genuine concern—Did your Alex know this Mary?—before organizing the great shows of grief displaying how Mary's death affected them. Like missing-person papers on light posts, monuments and testaments were not so much updated as posted, consulted, and read like tarot cards, as if the right web of information would not so much heal, but reveal some kind of truth.

With Mary being dead, no one except Mother knew everything. After the news broke, and on into the following days, it became clear to even Endwell's most ardent socialites that while much had been spoken of, nothing had been revealed. There had been a Freak Accident. An area student was dead. And that, at least for a while, was that.

But there is nothing if not time. And, in Endwell, there is not much by way of news to fill it. Above that fold, and beneath that headline, certain words—like accident, like category—assumed other meanings. Diction was not being read as intended. Syntax was skewed. And so those assuming vested interests misinterpreted intent, as if meaning had been exhumed from agenda's cemetery.

The problem wasn't syntactical. Or grammatical. What affected the community was a lofty, an almost elevated sort of ignorance. Words, employed to report, or to convey news, were not questioned to carry a fuller meaning. With everything being open to interpretation, the reporter's purpose was immediately denied distinction, and the reader assumed meanings' full weight. Sometimes what the author said as a statement of fact was questioned. Usually, though, readers defined not what any given word meant, but focused instead on the emotion, or sentiment, that they felt. That they inferred. The result being that inference was deemed more moderate; that supposition became the more plausible meaning. Very rarely did the opposite hold true. But more often than anything it was neither. In the end there was nothing. There existed no sufficient testimony in anything merely verbal.

Most people have trouble understanding information presented as column. They find such data difficult to consume. Like early readers, texts without pictures mean nothing. Consumers of images, here was a readership for whom black-and-white as adage wasn't a thing (how could this be when there was, for them, nothing by way of reality?) and language, like a photograph left in a vat for too long, bled to blur into a bloom of confusion, a world where it wasn't possible to introduce concepts like over- and underexposure without the corresponding images.

What does it say of Endwell that a positive of society was that it felt less badly and more intrigued? That victimhood presupposed a new sort of victimhood? One person—it doesn't matter who, she spoke for the city—tried to explain how she felt. She wrote The Endwell Standard. She was right. She was wrong. She was neither. In perception's frame, matted with the ignorance of long-held superstition trussed as belief, the Freak Accident should have incited compassion. And it did. But if justice is blind, ignorance is dumb. And offsetting compassion was a small, virulent, anathema. Mother was guilty, Endwell thought. Of what? Of disrupting their lives. For becoming a part of their lives.

What if the Freak Accident hadn't been a Freak Accident? What if, as many came to believe, investigators, in the absence of evidence (and given the fact that Jude was just a kid), shrugged, abdicated duty, and let his parents decide what to do?

While this was, more or less, true, no one could say so with certainty.

What was true?

To the answer of: What if Endwell knew?

The answer was this … A faction of the community would have grown incensed. And the core contingent of these agitators would have become even angrier, and this at a much faster rate, leaving, ironically, the second, and subsequent tragedy, without enough time to unfold.

At least probably.

Because backlash. Because an immediate public outcry would have blasted what remained of the Bendzes into some other position, into some other posture whose form would have assumed resignation, it being true that the Bendzes—and one of them, specifically—would have become far less comfortable leaving home until, after some particularly virulent threat—real or imagined—they opted against leaving their home altogether, the family then deciding to leave Endwell not as a means of forgetting, of starting over, but as a practical measure ensuring protection.

And who can be sure that Mary could have traveled? That Jude would have taken her with him?

And there was the funeral. All throughout the service (until its dramatic conclusion) when those in attendance thought Jude should be doing something reverent—like praying—and wondered how it could be that he wasn't crying, Endwell, horrified, wanted to speak, to shout, to say ...

The truth was, Jude had never seen a dead body. Following the Freak Accident, what happened had been so intense, what later happened had been so dramatic that, even though Mary visited Jude the day of her death, he had no way to deal with Mary's coffined corpse. He had done so little yet had exerted so much energy answering questions, and performing, and had received so much assurance, and had (even then) eaten so very little that it became possible for him to conceive of nothing other than getting away from Mary's dead body. Or of being with Mary's dead body. And so what happened then, his face smashed against a bed of roses, his arms wrapped around his sister's casket, was a sign. A warning.

Before Mary's coffin Jude remained motionless. Inert. Yesterday, he had seen Mary alive—or what he now thought of as her being dead. This had been much too different. A corpse was in the casket directly before him, but, like a mantle arranged in place to support Mary's portrait—a perfect likeness of Mary, and framed exclusively for this purpose, Endwell thought—and how, Jude thought, Mary seemed not animated, ready to speak, but dead. Fake. A flower inside a fallen tuxedo. A metaphor without comparison.

Not so much lost in thought as lacking process, Jude, too tired to realize that he was tired, his back and his abdomen sore from being so stressed, so tightly wound, wanted only to be somewhere else, to be left alone. The city misread him. Endwell ever looking and wondering, searching his expression for something, for anything, as if his face were not so much a map but a meme, offering nothing by way of direction but an element aligned with a culture currently constituted, proof of a behavior all can read and understand absent ambiguity or the requisite energy that accompanies thinking.

And his mother. Dressed as if ready for a wedding. For some other ceremony. Endwell already deep in its understanding that she was, in part, guilty of creating this atmosphere, this sadness within her son, this uncertainty.

And who enjoys feeling uncertain?

What do we make of others who force us to question our beliefs … Our convictions?

Ultimately, Endwell thought very little. Endwell thought next to nothing at all.

And how Helen appeared before Endwell, as pretty as a casket. Head straight, hair perfect and falling to her shoulders with conditioned iridescence, her blue eyes made bright by mascara, by a medicated emotional indifference. For her face—and Endwell had been watching—failed to register the agonies of her mind. Like Mary and Jude, her beauty and pain were separated from one another.

This enterprise upon which Endwell, together, would soon endeavor, had no precedent. There had been no "before." Once complete, there will only be "after." Their purpose? To examine—as if some sort of display—in every way, in every possible manner, both conceivable and true to nature, a child.

A child named Mary.

Endwell was simply itself. Only it knew not its heart. But that was okay. For Endwell understood itself. Endwell was made like every other person ever made. There are Endwells all over the world. This Endwell thought they were better than most, but they were no different, any more than all are the same.

Did Endwell do well or ill in casting the mold by which it would form Mary …

This is the question.

What followed was a resolution. Which, almost certainly, is no revelation.

AUGUST 15, 1983

August 15, 1983—a Monday—found Mother and Mrs. Kruty busily preparing for a Holy Day of Obligation. This left Jude, for the entirety of the afternoon, to his own devices. Had Mary been alive, and Jude still in school, the day would have proven unusual, given that this particular Monday informed the tail end of a rare, religious, hat trick.

First, per family tradition, Jude would have gone to church, Sunday morning, at ten-thirty. The next day—one of, according to Mother, the very most important days of the year—Jude, along with his class, would have attended a morning mass, a special in his academic schedule (in fact, Our Lady of the Lake, Boys, and Our Lady of the Lake, Girls, had just attended the service, an hour earlier). Lastly, in one more nod to the Virgin Mary, Jude, after Father got home from work, would have attended the seven o'clock service with his family. Because he wasn't attending school—was that why Mother had stopped at The Commons?—Jude had missed the morning service and avoided bumping into his classmates. Mother pointed them out, the boys in one line, the girls in the other, walking back to the building down the road, as she pulled into Our Lady of the Lake. This meant, like the weekend of the Freak Accident, Mother only expected Jude to attend mass twice.

Church, at night, was certainly strange, and more so when it wasn't winter. Evening blooming, the world cooled, and the sky assumed a beautiful black, shot through with that light offered by star and moon, a hallowed sort of illumination. Stepping from their pew and down the aisle, Jude and Mary would follow their parents, passing Father Hours and taking the steps to the sidewalk, the still air almost tropical and blending with their blood, adding texture to their skin, and how this felt as if stepping into a wonderful pool, or lagoon … some other Endwell far removed.

Yes, it certainly was strange to see Our Lady of the Lake at night. A measure of the construction's true beauty, the building's many windows giving, not receiving, it was as if the cathedral was carved from light itself, releasing this magic the same time every night, beams like tracers rising from some inner sanctum whose purpose was not to illuminate any one thing, but to demonstrate Man's awesome ability to create and to concentrate power.

Between the doors was a great stained-glass window, and yes, Mother—and Mrs. Kruty, too—were right: the window was beautiful. The window was mesmerizing. The window was two-sided so both those walking down the street and those praying inside the church saw the same image; so both the secular and the supplicant witnessed the same Jesus: a Jesus dressed in a simple white robe, the Son of God contained (like Mary) within a world of wild and wavering blues. His expression slightly bewildered. Or maybe ambiguous.

When it was sunny, or when the church was well-lit, Jesus would, for those walking down the street, their lines of vision shaking from the percussion of their footsteps, shimmer like that strata of heat visible above a city's summer street; just as, for those forlorn and destitute souls sitting upon their pews, the son of God projected from the window with the fractured force of some fantastic, holy hologram.

And then a bus would pass by and create beneath the concrete a little earthquake, and Jude, standing outside, would feel the ground move beneath his feet, waking him from his reverie. Dizzy, distracted, and unaware not of any one particular thought but of his body, that he was breathing, far off in the distance a train in its passing would wake him yet again and even Mom would turn, attuned, if not quite interested, to its crazed, its low-moaning horn. Jude's equilibrium pleasantly offset, he would follow his family to Dad's car. Mom, who, despite decades of daily religion, had developed no tolerance, would have been tipsy with that unique blend of piety, self-pleasure, and boisterous assurance that, along with the Holy Spirit, descended upon her with equal measure. On the drive home she would have directed their father to stop at Friendly's, for ice cream. Jude wouldn't have minded. He no longer knew how Mary would have reacted.

The weekend had been strangely cold, a mix of cloud and wind, fog and rain. Even the Sunday morning service had been subdued, and, for 1980s Endwell, poorly attended. So come Monday, when the sun seemed, of some special accord, to have risen early, giving way to so lovely a day, even Mother—whose baseline was never resting—was energized, and she roused Jude early, prattling on about Mary (the Saint), and the Mysteries of Faith, saying that she had to stop at The Commons to pick up a few items before heading to work.

Jude hadn't cared, asking only, during the drive, if he could sit outside, by the fountain, while Mother went shopping. Mother, always slow to allow anything by way of independence or agency, surprised Jude by saying "Yes." While there were rules—with Jude promising to do this, while agreeing to never to do that—and Mother selected the bench (an uncomfortable iron construction in the center of The Commons near the fountain), Jude, if nothing else, had a lot to look at. There was, at least, much to consider.

Elmira's scalloped hillsides blurred smokey blue against the early morning light, like long-ago flood lines marking some great calamity. Their trees still full of leaves, vibrant and laser-beam green (the city would enjoy an Indian Summer), tall pines in their clusters rose dark and rich as if to offer points of contrast. Off in the direction Mother had taken, the sign outside Endwell Band & Trust moved from seventy-nine to eighty degrees, and the air, free from humidity, devoid of breeze, confused birds and rattled bees, the insects rising and falling uncertainly before mindlessly buzzing, smacking into storefronts. In spirit, Jude, responsible for nothing, possessing no one reason for being, quietly celebrated a morning that evoked, of all things, a snow day.

There weren't many people to study, so Jude stared into the sky. Far above in that great distance a jet made to look tiny. Its contrail, huge in scale, fanning like a false breath to fluff into a "V" rich with definition and across the heavens dissipating, a series of chemical blasts thick like splatter paint, identifiable as blood splatter. Up there, where it was cool. Icy, even. Far below and to Jude's immediate north and south those neighborhoods surrounding The Commons, wide city streets with names like Elm and Oak, quiet as if compressed into an urban sort of silence by those different pressures occupying their huge old homes. Only here it wasn't cool, downtown Endwell being anything but ice. Front lawns, perfect squares usually verdant, their fat blades of grass lustrous, as if injected with a sort of collagen green, were sun-blanched and dead, or dying, blocks of deadpan so far gone that no amount of water, of falling rain, could save them. Like those impatiens in their window boxes, the geraniums on their stoops in their terra cotta pots. How their petals, crisp as cornflakes and black as scabs, ran red only occasionally, and this only the result of some random event, or occasion—ordinary accidents—as a fresh scratch wells stoplight bright upon a child's pale arm.

Yes, it was hot. Afternoon was boring into morning, sunshine beating Endwell's cool, lemon-yellow daylight into submission and below the city's gentle, rolling hillsides the day's new-formed sky streamed like steam to assume a stratum the soft and porous blue of a surgeon's mask. And so a suggestion of clouds when there were none. A depth of color atop color that became a federal sort of firmament, a rich plumb suggesting if not the beginning of outer space than the end of some inner atmosphere, an ambiguous and undefined purgatory silently bleeding into the vacuum of its own base simplicity.

Jude closed his eyes. He placed the plane above a home not far from Mother and Father's, a residence blanked by the browning elevation of the great pine rising upon what once passed for a front yard. Mother hated the place. The lawn's fall giving way to a staircase about half collapsed beneath the weight of some forgotten season's buoyant grapevine, about the only living thing living and doing so just to strangle that which supported it, lent if life. The woody vines spiraling tight as a fist to form like so many suffocating crowns something like a simile, it leaves desiccated and withered and mottled black, the vine writhing as if in abject agony, all of it twisted, most of it dead, that which survived slinking, creeping along the deadpan as if to escape itself, to form some new, better self, tendrils and claspers reaching out like the desperate hands of so many drowning men towards the blackened agony of a Cape Myrtle, a blast of beauty erupting from this dead and fissured earth.

Jude loved it.

Atop the staircase a wide wooden stoop sagging like a dock falling into a forgotten pond, and how—at least when Jude imagined it—there was always a cat in its perch upon this fractured edifice, a cat cleaning its ears. Licking its curled, calloused paw the cat, head turned, worked its paw against an ear, its whiskers. And the cat pausing now, her forepaw drawn to her mouth, this cat the color of a used cigarette filter, the tip of its tail withered, and how the cat, ever arrested, looked down from the sinking stoop, its yellow eyes greening and locked, its body tense. Behind the animal the door opened and a man—Mary would have known how to describe him—stepped from the house and with a struck match lit something to smoke. With feline grace the cat fell from the stoop to slide beneath the steps, a liquid movement, like a sheet of paper falling from a desk to the floor.

Our Lady of the Lake called the quarter hour. The heat settled. The sun, high overhead, a perfect circle. There was so much light. Dogs and even cats moved only to purchase greater plots of shade, tongues lolling, limbs splayed, their bellies so exposed like sockets pulling coolness from the planet's ready reserves. Mother, a few shops away, called Jude's name. The sound grew in frequency. In urgency. As if she couldn't see him and was growing worried. As if they were in some sort of hurry.

Inside the tower, high atop Our Lady of the Lake, it was dark and cool, the atmosphere the same as it had been that first morning Jude followed Mary up the stairs. The airplane long gone, having landed at Endwell Airport, or, if it had just that morning taken off, heading for some other, bigger city, like New York, or Los Angeles. Downstairs, far below, Mother and Mrs. Kruty were decorating Our Lady of the Lake's baptismal fountain, draping the area with blue fabrics and placing on the floor and the space's few pedestals huge white lilies, their pots wrapped in shiny gold foil. They worked quietly, almost competitively. Jude didn't care for either woman, particularly. When they were together, it was like being at school, observing and taking in the casual cruelty kids effortlessly inflicted upon one another.

The Commons' fountain, with its artificial water (a base compound infused with so many chemicals that the water appeared thicker, even heavier), the display—its basin glittering the copper and gold of tossed pennies, those wishes cast in the way of prayer—spurt huge plumes of water Kool-Aid blue. These, in their carefully articulated bursts, achieved the exact same apexes before collapsing in upon themselves. These, despite the garishness of such artificial substance, were pretty—there being beauty in movement, in this manufactured symmetry. And how in decades this fountain, like that fountain inside Our Lady of the Lake (an ugly, overly ornate construction, large enough to hold a dozen babies), while maintained, will largely be forgotten. Its plumbing broken beyond repair, the construction, filled every year not with water but flowers, with annuals, with bright red geraniums and impatiens pink, white, striped, yellow, and purple, and tall green thrillers like coleus, and for added color vibrant flowers like Butterfly argyranthemum (so bright, so yellow), and pale green ivy spiraling—from the top of the fountain a variety of ivies cascading down the tiers to rest upon flower petals and the damp soil contained within the wide basin beneath; spiraling down upon the ground, their leaves crushed by people passing by.

Nearby, four concrete chairs. Like petrified toadstools these rose from the bricks. A false nature. And sculpted atop one of the chairs a life-like woman. Concrete, this woman. Less alive than Mary, sitting with legs crossed at the heels, a petite, concrete businesswoman, replete in pants suit and high heels, her concrete smile tight-lipped and bemusing, her hair styled in a severe, concrete flip, her eyeglasses dramatic, like cat's eyes making strange her face. The concrete woman contemplated a cup of coffee—a cup of coffee held between two concrete hands, concrete hands with long, perfectly manicured fingernails—and how the concrete cup of coffee was half empty, the cup of coffee and the hands with their concrete fingernails and the concrete wrists and concrete cuffs at rest upon the table and all of this a mossy green … the concrete woman and the concrete coffee green with moss, covered with a dusting of plant life, and this green sculpture glowing, the green sculpture glowing with a fine, thin mist of moss, of life, and the green of this moss evanescent, glowing, as if lit by some internal source unseen.

Motionless, like that light which fills an open door, Mary marked the end, or the beginning, of the church's spiral staircase, that construction which, according to Mother, would be here long after Jude was gone.

"Jude," Mary said. "Trust me. Your mind. It is whole. It is one with your body. What your body has been telling you is a lie, and you now know this. You have overcome what is needed. Your life is now yours. Not Mother's. But yours." Mary flickered. She continued. "Like your body, your life is yours to inhabit, or to leave. It is your body, and it is your choice. Only you can end your suffering. This is what freedom means."

Sunlight and sky made the tower's west-facing window a plane as blue and as still as Cascadilla Lake, a color, once concentrated, that erased Mary's eyes. Such queer geometry. Jude raised a hand to create a shadow, or an odd sort of mirror, and he was right—Mary's eyes materialized. As her eyes arrived, her face, outlined by her radiant, brown hair, came more fully into focus. Her high cheekbones, her full lips, each feature, like a charcoal etching, both blurry and sharply defined. He lowered his hand. Her eyes disappeared.

Her face erased. Such simple cause and effect. He thought of the pond. He wondered if Mary knew that Mother had left him alone, by the fountain, and if this was why she seemed agitated. Bothered. That he had never thought to augment her shape, or appearance, was significant—the oversight adding to the day's growing list of misgivings. Add to this ominous inventory the promise that his sister was whiter than ever and that, consequently, she looked more ghostly, more ghoulish, too? While Jude could not exactly figure the pattern, or formulate the equation, something, Jude knew, was going to change. It was as though he (there was no other way to explain it) was going to happen.

Jude took the last few steps. Walking around Mary—he still didn't think it possible to pass through her—he approached the altar, fingered a wick, and pushed a fingernail into its candle. Like so much of his world, a world whose margins Mother, and, to a greater degree, Mary, defined, the wax was smooth and cool. Of course Mary had insisted they visit the tower. She was always pushing Jude to visit the tower.

Whatever.

Jude no longer cared. Getting caught? Didn't matter. As point of fact, pretty much nothing—if you thought about it—mattered. At least not really. In being dead, Mary illustrated this. Say Jude was caught. Discovered. Would this offense, one year from today, amount to anything? Unlikely. Look at Mother. She had killed a little kid. His sister. Mother's own daughter. And what was she doing now? She certainly wasn't sitting in prison. She certainly didn't seem sad. And she didn't act guilty, either. Nope. Mother was playing with flowers. She ironed sheets for Our Lady of the Lake's altar.

Say Jude was caught. While there would be immediate fallout—with Mother doing something dramatic and stupid, like crying—would this offense, one year from today, amount to anything? The answer, almost certainly, was no. Unless someone (like Mother, or some therapist) went looking to remember those things Jude had done wrong, tallying, then recording, with recounted transgressions functioning like how notches on a basement door frame make up a growth chart, today, like almost every other day, would be forgotten, lost within the swamp of time informing his particular existence.

"Mother. And not just her, but people. By nature they are so busy living that only those events tied to meaningful outcomes occupy anyone's mind – anyone's memory. They all spend more time planning, or imagining, or simply existing, rather than remembering, let alone considering, time past and whatever had happened. And they never remember anything good."

Mary sounded just like Father Hours. Jude tried to picture him, there, where Mary stood. But he could not. He was unable to. As if reading his mind she continued, repeating something she had heard ...

"Like swords we draw upon memories only when interested in wielding them as weapons to wound one another, or to inform the stakes supporting our scarecrows of self-righteousness."

Even Mary, being dead—no matter Mother's fixation with the present—moved through, or with, time. Not that Jude was particularly looking, but, other than her ability to sound like Father, or Father Hours, he failed to see much of a difference. She continued.

"Remember when Father Hours once preached that any idiot could toss a tiny pebble into the middle of Cascadilla Lake?"

Jude wished she would imitate Father Hours, but she was either incapable of changing her voice, or didn't find it necessary.

"Gather one hundred of the smartest people to ever walk the planet," he said. "Call upon whomever you like and give them one hundred years and if they happened to find the rock—they won't—it would be an accident. He was talking about us, Jude. He was talking about Mother."

Jude remembered.

More likely, Father Hours said, these people – who we label paralegal and professor, politician and philosopher – would, instead of looking, of seeking, devise plans, ways, or systems of looking. They would surface from the depths of their ideas dry and empty handed.

"We think, when we should be asking. We seek, when we should be listening," Mary said. "Mother, for all her talk of Father Hours, of God, wants you to forget. She wants Endwell to forget. And they will. Unless we. Unless you remind them."

Consider the years of all the generations. Ask your father, and he will inform you. Ask the elders, and they will tell you. Ask me, and I'll ask you this: Why would we even bother searching for something a fool has thrown?

Jude may not have cared for Father Hours—although he was growing to like the man—he liked what the priest had to say. He took his work, as opposed to himself, seriously. His homilies made common sense, and he colored his content with pop culture references and humorous anecdotes. Jude most respected the priest's commitment to caring, that he led by example, and how he experienced such obvious pain when understanding that his parishioners weren't listening. He knew what it was like, not being heard.

Jude wasn't looking for anything. If anything, he hoped to forget. He didn't need anyone's help with that. He wanted to pass through existence with Mary—whatever that might mean—waiting for the day things got better. And things could get better, if Mary allowed for it.

He could even—though he willed this thought away, fearing Mary might catch on—imagine an existence without Mary. It was not as though he would ever forget her. In his memory—and in many other ways—she would be more alive to him than she was now. He could construct her. And his version of Mary, while partly ghostly, would mostly be the Mary he remembered from before the Freak Accident—not this ghoulish simulation. As day erased day, this became more difficult. As if part of Mary's purpose in being dead was to make sure Jude forgot who she had been while alive. When living.

What concerned Jude, presently, was people. Company. Disheveled classmates. Little boys whose wrinkled shirts and unkempt hair belied his school's attempt to present as image a neatly assembled and manicured collection of children shimmering with faith, newly confirmed (or soon to be), and, so minted, pressed fresh as new currency.

This present is his outline, and this does not change if Jude is home or if he is at school. But when at Endwell Children's his drawings revealed another dimension, for they were complex and mysterious, and they will, like Mary, live to haunt Endwell long after all that happens. The clue within his drawings is that they come from the mind of a very unhappy child. Often they are less drawing than dialogue; transcripts from those conversations he held with himself. Inside a prison, inside a zoo, here is Jude presented so violently that suicidal is not too severe a conclusion for a nurse or a caseworker to draw, and yet the feeling of his own, overwhelming fear—evident there in his childhood creations—remained hidden from those who looked, but did not see.

Jude's life unfolded before Endwell, a people who, as spectators, were an active, at times incendiary, audience. Marionettes, not martinets, Endwell watched with metered absorption as the acts of the play propelled themselves like a monsoon.

But really, it just seemed that way. Jude was alone. No one cared. Mother and Father not present (or unwilling) to make sense of the strangeness that flooded his life, every action took its birth in him, and their consequences were felt by Jude alone.

Those few figures who, from the beginning, should have stood with him, acted without thinking. Before long they, like Mary, faded, as if terrified of some unseen thing. The boy with the dead twin was condemned to speak, to struggle, to suffer, alone.

Jude communicated with no one.

And no one had anything to say.

Most of us know how to avoid danger; how to keep ourselves healthy, well, and, if not happy, intact. Did Jude court danger? Invite discontent? While doctors and psychiatrists were quick to sweep an impressionable boy off into a gulf of shame and disgust, they were, also, capable of bringing him back to shore. To purity.

Why didn't they?

Not even they could say.

But time does nothing if not pass, and life after the calm afforded by his time alone was quickly becoming unbearable.

He would wake, following eternity after eternity of trying to fall asleep, shocked, and dismayed, not to feel himself alive in his cool, moonlit honeycomb, but that, like a rat in a cage, he was at Mother's house, in a bed, the door to his room open, every part of him exposed.

And this, in part, was Mary's doing. Her fault. Her responsibility.

He was grateful.

He was indebted to Mary for his survival—when he thought about it (which, too, was not often)—he couldn't imagine how his life would have unfolded if she hadn't appeared that night, after they had returned from the hospital. Thanks to Mary, he had carved for himself a truly charmed existence. While he never believed that he was sick, it was easy to feel that he wasn't well. Until the very end he never thought of himself as a burden, that he needed looking after …

And to the degree that he was, he was easier to care for than the other kids—boys and girls his age (and older) who cut themselves or starved themselves skinny or set fires or even injured animals. He had made the nurses' lives easier! They hadn't wanted him to go. Even Mother had not wanted him to go. Relieved, she enjoyed, with her living child hospitalized, a certain sort of freedom. And whenever she felt low, and needed attention? Well, she simply had to mention Jude, or in some way suggest that he was on her mind, and poof! As if a heady elixir, she had, from her friends and the ladies at Our Lady of the Lake, a steady stream of attention, a pool of platitudes and I'm-so-sorry's in which she could cleanse. In which she could bathe. Transform. And in her way, on her terms, become born again.

Jude wasn't scared of Mother. He knew that, due to his own behavior, she would never have a reason, accidentally or otherwise, to harm him. Just like he knew—because of Mary's behavior—that Mother had not woken up planning to hurt her. Angry, in that one moment (and Mary was being annoying, even Jude had thought so) Mother, while wrong, had just wanted to punish her, to get Mary to live the way Mother wanted her living. Hurting Mary until she died was not Mother's idea of better. It just wasn't. What happened was as random (maybe even more so) as Mary and Jude being born, from inside her, to begin with. Like Father Hour's idiot, or the idiot's stone, they could relive that Christmas morning one hundred times, and there would be one hundred different outcomes, and almost certainly none of them would end with Mary being found dead; conversely, it was far more likely that every scenario would find the family attending mass.

"You're right not to worry about Mother," Mary said. As if pushed, she drifted from the steps, towards Jude. "But you are wrong, too."

Jude did not feel like unraveling one of Mary's riddles. Right or wrong, his answers made no difference.

"Jude," Mary said. "Father Hours. Mother. They are ready to tell you all about God. The mysteries of faith. Of those two, who do you think tells more of the truth?"

"Father Hours," Jude said.

Mary did not nod, and she did not blink. She said, "And why do you think that is?"

Ignoring Mary or answering her endless questions: both were a form of exercise; both were exhausting, difficult in their own ways. Jude also knew that Mary wanted him to believe he arrived at the conclusion that mother was a liar, and a phony, independently. Jude had no idea why. While never as much as Mary, or with such severity, Jude knew this about Mother already. What he found more interesting than anything was that Father Hours, a priest, a man married to God the way Mother was married to Father, seemed to believe less in Jesus, seemed less interested in religion than mother, yet still had more faith.

Mother could never be a priest. But if Mother loved and believed in God so much she could have become a nun. Only—and this became more evident every day—there was a limit to what she was willing to sacrifice. She wanted a little bit of everything. She lived her life as though it—existence—were not a gift, but that she was the present. It was so confusing. But it didn't have to be. Mother would never believe in Mary. Father Hours? He could. He might not say as much out loud, and certainly not to someone like Mother, but the priest was more than words. He questioned what he couldn't see. He was interested. And that had to mean something.

Mary was not gone. And how this, too, meant something. Mainly, Jude reasoned, that there was more to living, or being dead, than living with Mother and Father, or coming and going from school. Mary wasn't Jesus, but her being here, now, made of living—of being dead—a certain sort of sense. This sort of sense was difficult to make in a world where kids are told not to just sit there, but to do something. But maybe Father Hours saw Jesus—his Ghost—just like Jude saw Mary. Only a little bit differently. Not that this much mattered. If Jude could count on anything to hold true it was that living, here, involved Mother, and that living here, with Mother, meant (however eventually, it was going to happen) going to school—and feeling scared and tired and uncomfortable and terrible. He was only uncertain about one thing.

"But what about Dad," Jude said.

"Father?"

"Yeah," Jude said. "Won't he be sad? Won't he—"

Since the Freak Accident, Jude could not remember thinking about his father. Occasionally, Father entered his dreams. And, occasionally, Jude thought back to Christmas, how he had acted—how he had looked—with Mary, dead, or dying, blue on the kitchen floor. But that was it. He had forgotten that his father was polite to the detectives. Jude—if only because he blocked that morning from his mind—did not remember his father trying, and failing, to pull him from Mary's coffin. Father had been more of a ghost than Mary; in being dead, Mary was still more alive than he was. Jude was not angry, exactly. And he did not blame his father for making things worse. But, and his eyes welled with tears, and his throat burned, what was true was that his father did nothing to make things better.

"That is something only you can consider," Mary said. She flickered. Nothing atop Our Lady of Sorrows brightened. Just Mary. His sister. "He is not guilty ..."

Like a leaf, pushed by the breeze, she moved from the chamber and down a hall. She passed through a doorway and disappeared. Made of light, it was as though she had none to spare, and so emitted no glow, that spot she once inhabited black. Like everything with Mary, it was all or nothing. And if Jude wanted to hear her, he had to follow. And Jude wanted to hear her. So he found himself further from the spiral staircase than ever before when she appeared, stopped, and said, "But he is not innocent, either."

Before, Jude had no desire to explore the tower. This apathy had been replaced by a curiosity more to do with discovering aspects of Mary, than looking about areas atop Our Lady of the Lake. Like Mother many years before him, Jude had believed that the tower, and the top of the church, generally, were under construction. Having now visited the space more times than he could recall, it was evident that aside from what Mary had planned, nothing atop Our Lady of the Lake was underway. Father Hours might not have meant to lie, but, in truth, he had. Upstairs, passageways and entire wings were no doubt dangerous. But contractors were not working to preserve anything.

Jude didn't know where they were. He was unsure how he had managed to walk so great a distance in such complete and total darkness. He had not realized he had been dragging his hands along the walls. His knuckles were sore. And bleeding. He brought a hand to his mouth and tasted blood. He bit the ragged bits of torn flesh.

"Just imagine what you can do," Mary said.

Her blue eyes bright, her dark hair framed her thin, pale face. "Jude," Mary said. "Remember what I told you? To trust me? Well, you have. And it has happened. Your mind. It is whole. It is one with your body. Look. You didn't even bring a flashlight. You have overcome what was needed. Whatever happens from this point forward, you have set yourself free."

Once, when they were younger, Mother and Father had taken them to Howe Caverns. The popular tourist attraction had nothing to do with Our Lady of the Lake, so even Mary was excited. The tour began with an elevator ride several stories beneath the surface. Many steps and carefully maintained paths wound for almost a mile above a river that spun into a great underwater lake. They rode canoes atop the black water until they reached a man-made construction protecting visitors from a dramatic waterfall. Before they turned in their seats for the ride back, the guides turned off the cave's lightning. The depth of the darkness was so total people gasped and young children cried. When the experience was over, and their guides had turned on the lights, Jude noticed that the scared young children had closed their eyes, that they had buried themselves into their parents. He thought of that now. A child's instinct to combat fear, to combat darkness, with more darkness.

Here, above the church, Jude listened. He peered into the blackness and knew this to be complete and total. He understood that Mary was taking him somewhere he hadn't before been. He tried to study the darkness. What was black seemed to move, to swirl like mist. Like smoke. But Jude knew this couldn't be so.

"Interesting, no?"

Mary's eyes were so bright. Only in them there was nothing to see. And Jude believed that, even as she looked at him, she didn't look to see. That, like a rag doll, she may as well have had stitches for eyes. He wanted to ask her. Again. He wanted to know what it was like. Being dead. He wanted her to explain everything. Or at least one thing. What she wanted. Why she was still here.

"Let me tell you a story. Okay?"

Mary. Of course in telling him something, she would raise some sort of question. Or lesson. And how in this way she was no different than anyone else in his life. Including Mother. But Jude buried his thoughts. He didn't want Mary to hear them. He listened to her story about Sister Robert Rita … He drifted …

When she had finished, Jude nodded. He knew. He understood. Everything. There was only one thing that remained unclear. He had never weighed notions concerning luck. Or fate—the heart of Mary's story. But there was a part of him, and he stepped towards his sister …

Maybe most of Jude knew that he was acting, not deciding. That what happened, and he reached for Mary, would be decided for him. And that because of this not even God would find him guilty.

Of course Jude passed through Mary!

Mary was no more something to hold than a figment of his imagination was anything other than an idea to consider. His sister would have had more substance were she a piece of paper, and Jude had drawn her. But what Jude did see, his foot, his body's full weight buckling the floor and then breaking through the ceiling (the area was so rotted that when they found him—and then later examined his body—he was, other than misaligned from one or two major injuries, largely unmarked; on his arms and on his legs there were no scrapes and no cuts—it was, the coroner later remarked, as if he had simply jumped into an empty swimming pool), was a great, white light.

Or great white lights.

MOMENTS BEFORE

Passing through Mary, Jude leaned to look through the hole in the ceiling—although it was possible he was falling, already—and, seeing the altar below, free from the cathedral's stained-glass shadows and so an incredibly bright white, he was overcome with happiness.

The altar was simple and beautiful. From Jude's perch atop the cathedral's canopy, it seemed as if Our Lady of the Lake had been built around the structure—a wooden A-shaped base—and how this seemed an extension of the floor, an instrument carved from an ancient walnut tree whose roots still ran beneath the carpeted steps to reach towards the wealth of water afforded by Cascadilla Lake. Once felled, craftsmen carved the mighty walnut's stump into that which nature cannot create—a perfect triangle— two clean lines rising to inform a point so perfect it took Jude's breath away.

If his life did, indeed, pass before his eyes, life was not some past, or future, now. Falling—or just about to—Jude was, like anyone living, completely alive. So why would objects appear differently? It wasn't like he was driving, looking into some side view mirror. Still living, Jude, like anyone, possessed memory. And it struck him how, many months ago, he had been sitting in the nursery, and how he saw the altar, and how what he saw arrived as a sort of insight (as opposed to realization); that what his Mother had arranged really was pretty, the cloth more white that anything—but how there was that bit of purple, too—and so for that alone maybe some of what Mother did had purpose, wasn't just some hyper-crazed posturing extravagance.

After—or as—Jude fell, he saw candles. Like the lights in his hospital room, they looked like something above him; apertures embedded in great gilded holders that he could, had he the time, count. And how atop and around the altar the dozens upon dozens of candles and the flowers—there were great, white flowers, glowing bright like strung Christmas lights from within their foil-wrapped pots—shimmered like stars. As if Jude were not falling but stepping into space. And this created calm. Great peace.

From so airy a height (Jude was definitely falling, there was no other way to explain the way he now viewed the world, how he was able to bend his line of vision as easily as darkness covers light) the walnut altar, finished with a catalyzed lacquer, a synthetic sort of bark protecting the wood from water and other stains that, when candlelit, shimmered with a subdued sort of psychedelia. The altar seemed to breathe. A gentle rise and fall that suggested an animal resting.

Yes. Jude knew the altar well.

Falling …

Falling, Jude began to feel colder, and he remembered, he saw one afternoon when his mother said something about him needing exercise, that she was worried about him spending so much time alone, and how she was going to take him on a tour, how it was one thing to hear about the altar, but another to visit the artwork, to see the marvel up close …

Considering the altar, Jude felt a gentle resistance, the surety that his fall—which of course would eventually terminate—was coordinated with what he saw, and what he thought, and that he still had time, perhaps plenty of time, because the altar was still quite far away, and there was still much to consider. He was going to strike the altar—there was nothing he could do to prevent that—so why worry? The more he remembered, the more time he had to fall. The more he fell, the more time he had to remember.

The altar looked nothing like it did now, blazing with its blues and whites, glowering with its oversized flowers and candles in their huge holders. Flowers that, because Jude was falling, became brighter. Candles that, because Jude was falling, loomed larger. Best not to think about that. Better not to think but to recall. To remember.

That afternoon with Mother, Jude had been struck by the plainness of it all, how the altar looked like the bottom of a creek bed come summer when the water ran so low it had been possible for him and Mary to walk great distances without passing so much as a puddle. That it was so natural. Even mass could be made more interesting if Father Hours operated from something simpler.

Naturally, the space between Jude and the altar had, through the course of this most recent reminiscence, greatly diminished. There wasn't much time. He didn't try to answer the foe that was gravity, for the force just was—and even if it wasn't, it's not as though gravity had asked him a question. Perhaps Jude had already smacked the altar face first (he was looking west, towards the great wooden doors) and saw sprayed, like ketchup, his blood. Although he didn't think the word "blood" or about "blood" but, rather, of roses, of the story Mary had just told him. And how, in one of her strange ways, she had managed to both harm and help him.

A woman, much older—Jude had seen her many times before, with her head, like a limp nimbus, wrapped in a worn blue bandana—was inside the church, head lowered, praying. Mary sat beside her. So pretty. More white than strange. The old woman's voice floated up to great him:

"O Blessed Mother Assumed into Heaven, after years of heroic martyrdom on earth, we rejoice that you have at last been taken to the throne prepared for you in Heaven by the Holy Trinity / Lift our hearts with you in the glory of your Assumption above the dreadful touch of sin and impurity / Teach us how small earth becomes when viewed from heaven / Make us realize that death is the triumphant gate through which we shall pass to your Son and that someday our bodies shall rejoin our souls in the unending bliss of heaven / From this earth, which we tread as pilgrims …"

Finished, she pointed at Jude. To highlight, if only to herself, what was happening.

She dropped her rosary.

Jude watched the red beads slide from her old slender fingers and heard not so much that they clattered—they had—but settled.

Things were really happening, now.

The story Mary had just told him, though. That which moved him to hug her, to forget that she might not fully be there. That he'd only end up disappointed. He had not known what Mary meant, but he understood … he could tell that something was different. Her words seemed to come from some other place. Not here—which was to say Earth—but from some place deep inside her, a voice that confirmed what Jude knew to be true. Falling, Jude didn't have much time. He used a hand to push away hair that had fallen in front of his face.

No.

He didn't have much time. Jude was plenty alive to know that much.

But he wanted to know what Mary had meant.

Sister Robert Rita held the flower like a microphone, Mary had said.

Silenced, Mary flickered, and in that passing light Jude saw a smile.

A strange story, Jude hoped that caring enough to puzzle out its meaning would allow for more time falling. Of falling, though, he again saw the altar. Its candles and coverlet. The mensa. The flowers. The side and front drops. And he heard—he was that much closer now— water surging from Our Lady of the Lake's baptismal fountain.

He saw Mary flicker. He saw her smiling. And in that smile he was unsure if he saw sadness. Or happiness.

Maybe both …

Meanwhile, looking directly before him, Jude grew less confident. He was no longer self-assured. He felt his heart beating, and while he knew that he didn't jump—or at least he didn't think so—he couldn't escape the idea that he had made a terrible mistake. If he had learned anything from the Freak Accident it was that fear was powerful. And that you could make mistakes that had no remedy. But, and he took comfort from this, at least he had not hurt anybody. He had escaped from the nightmare of that particular existence and no longer had to fear confinement, or imprisonment … he was free.

The water from the baptismal fountain burst not so much like a sound, but a sight—a firework far above him, its release mercury, and silver, and symmetrically perfect.

Jude did know that the altar was, in fact, growing larger. Sadly, this didn't require much by way of thinking, and did not slow his fall. The candles surrounding the altar created a great halo. Giving up on the story, he tried to think of something—of anything—but this seemed to activate gravity, so he allowed his mind to drift to his life's most horrible memory, Mary's funeral, and how there were long black cars and other cars and how they stopped and men and women slowly rose out of them and how they were in no hurry to go.

He seemed to smell the colors of the women's glittering jewelry, and he felt above the coffin the stolid weight of Our Lady of the Lake's cross. Jude had never minded Jesus hanging there most Sundays, but for Mary's funeral? Jesus should have been taken down. The day was about Mary. Mother had dressed as if for a party, and of course it was impossible to arrive late, to be anything but early. Father was clearing his throat and Jude had sat down between them wondering if Mary was actually inside the coffin—he had wondered if anyone had actually checked.

When Mary hadn't appeared he knew he was alone. Life was a contest, and he had not won. Sweat ran down a thigh. He had hated that suit. Looking behind him he saw one detective, and then he looked until he found the other. They had wanted something from him, only Mary would not let him give. Closing his eyes, the wind of his weight rushing to meet him, he knew this now. Being dead, Mary only took.

What would have happened if he had told them everything? He tried to think harder, to think deeper, but he was running out of time. His ears filled with the sound of running water and he could smell flowers and feel heat from the lit candles and he was so close now that all he saw was his imagination—whatever was in his mind. And this was white.

Before him already the first crimson flash—it was not a poinsettia—like a flower's leaf, spreading. He looked for Mary, but no, she was not there, she was gone, waiting.

And Jude kissed the altar. His head, as if a summons, singing like a struck bell.

Moments Before (Within), and Once Upon a Time (Without)

Sister Robert Rita held the rose like a microphone. We, she said, are just as lovely. We are soft evening skies, our hopes and dreams rising low to form full, sun-kissed clouds, dark silver outlines aging against an azure forever rising to erase its own base simplicity. Ordinary tragedies, we'll burst, our showers falling to the earth warm as tears, pounding the concrete. Until we evaporate. Until, individually, we are nothing, once more.

We.

Sister's young ladies.

None of whom in this, the end of our first century, care to put off living, any more than we could hold off breathing. Yet how she tended to us there, within her dreary, dusty classroom, which she brightened with small, personal effects—a framed picture of St. Stephen, and a photo of her best friend with a hand grenade at Mardi Gras—understanding understatement in ways that we noticed and appreciated and valued in a world where the sweetness of the rose relies upon the name she wears.

You are this flower. Sister smiled. During this exercise, you, while holding the rose, with the others looking on, are this rose. You, while looking on, your friends holding the flower, remain this rose. This is all you need to understand. No questions.

We. Wearing our uniforms—those maroon skirts, white shirts, and sensible shoes. Most of us braided our hair or pulled our hair into ponytails with worn rubber bands. Our shirts weren't very white, and the maroon had faded to assume some other, nameless, color. We grew like weeds, and so it was not the clothing, it was we who looked disheveled, like broken and rejected mannequins.

We were in grade school and so lipstick wasn't okay.

There was no such thing as a touch of mascara.

We wore white knee socks.

Our backpacks identified us.

But those they locked away.

Sister handed the rose to Tanya. The rose was erect, its leaves alternate and feathery, its sharply-toothed leaflets firm and oval. Cultivated, it was the red of Mother's lipstick, the blood from a nose, and the rose had rows and rows of petals, a floral chalice firm, as if compressed by gentle hands. This wasn't the point, but most of us had never really held a rose, and it was difficult to remember who we were, and what Sister wanted us to be, in the presence of this strange and sudden beauty.

We weren't too old as to no longer vie for turns, or to resent alphabetical order, but we respected Sister and even if we didn't we knew that class goes on not so much without us, but with her. After a minute she told Tanya to pass the flower to someone, to anyone, in class.

Surprise.

This was how Sister worked. We should have known better. There, at our desks, we didn't like freedom, we didn't want choice, and Tanya turned, she handed the rose to Alicia, the girl behind her.

Ah, Sister had said, I should have mentioned. The only stipulation is that you leave your seats. The lesson is

interactive, ladies. And, of course, no talking. But that—
she smiled—goes without saying.

Tanya pushed up from her desk. In doing so, she bent the
flower's stem. Water beaded from the tear as Tanya, smiling,
sashaying, made to pass the flower to her best friend, before
pivoting, and handing the flower to Susanne.

Susanne wasn't ready. Pricked, the flower fell to the
floor. Fuck.

Sister fought only so many battles. She nodded, then
said, Pick it up.

Sucking a finger, Susanne twirled the flower. We knew
that a minute was a long time, but we never got used to that
feeling. When directed, Susanne stood, took two steps, and
passed the flower to Tamra. Wary, Tamra pinched the rose
by a few petals, her fingers slick with oil, and the rose
loosened, and the room filled with perfume.

Things are not only what they are, they were, in
important respects, what they seemed to be. What elixir,
what camphor did the world have to offer Brighton? Or
Tori, when it was her turn to hold the flower? There is
hope for a painter when she doesn't have a canvas, Sister
told us, at least once a week.

And then, The magic is not in the painting, it's in
devising, and then creating, the hope.

That time can move both fast and slow?

This is amazing, Jude.

In seven minutes the bell was going to ring, and that is
when Gyllian returned the rose.

Ladies, Sister Robert Rita said. She held the flower, sadly.
And then she said, Sustained silent writing. To the best of
your ability, please describe this rose. I'd prefer that you
discuss its condition, but we're short on time. No questions.

We picked up our pencils. We wondered what to write.
Toes curled, hands clenched, we considered the flower.
And we wrote what we saw.

What we didn't write was that, desiccated, the rose drooped, as if ashamed. Its leaves had lost their agency, and a few, like shed shirts, had fallen on the floor. When Sister altered her grip, no longer securing the stem where the tear, in time, extended, and now looked flattened, shredded, pale green strands bent as the flower flopped.

We gasped.

We wrote about thorns. We wrote how the rose smelled pretty. We used the word red. We used the word green. We didn't mention soft. We couldn't, in one word, describe vulnerability.

But five minutes later? With Sister and the rose at the head of the room?

We were still writing, and that bell still rings.

CONTENT WARNINGS

Abuse
Child endangerment
Death or dying
Eating disorders
Mental illness
Suicide or self-inflicted harm

ACKNOWLEDGEMENTS

John McManus, Luisa Igloria, Janet Peery, Sherri Reynolds, Kent Wascom, Rebecca Bengal, Elizabeth Groeneveld, Manuela Mourao, Timothy Fulghum, Wendel Ward, my parents, my other parents: Ricky and Catherine, Dan, Phinneas, Charlie, Jewel, Zz, and Solomon.

About the Author

Richard Leise is the author of the acclaimed fictions Inter Alia and Next To Nothing. A Perry Morgan Fellow from Old Dominion University, he lives, writes, and teaches in New York with his wife and twins. This is his first novel. He is @coy_harlingen on Twitter.

More from Brigids Gate Press

A tragic accident, shrouded in mystery, leads to a family reunion in the hidden village of Little Hatchet, located in the smothering shadow of GodBeGone Wood, the home of the mythical Woodcutter and Grandma. Alec Eades rediscovers his bond with GodBeGone Wood and the future his father agreed to years ago as nefarious landowner Oliver Hayward schemes to raise money for the village by re-enacting part of the Woodcutter legend. Old wounds are reopened and ties of blood and friendship are tested to the extreme when the Woodcutter is summoned and Grandma returns.

Something is outside; in the fields, by the ditches, on the roads. Something old and cruel and vicious. When Luke Sheridan moves out of Dublin city to rural Kilcross with his wife and baby, he imagines the worst part will be his extended commute to work. They can look forward to enjoying the countryside and being part of a small community. After all, his old friend Declan Maguire lives in the house next door and is a Garda in the nearest town. But Declan's devilish attitude towards drink, drugs and women means trouble is never far from his door. And worse, gruesome murders and the appearance of sinister figures at night mean the countryside is becoming a very dangerous place to live. Country Roads—don't go outside alone.

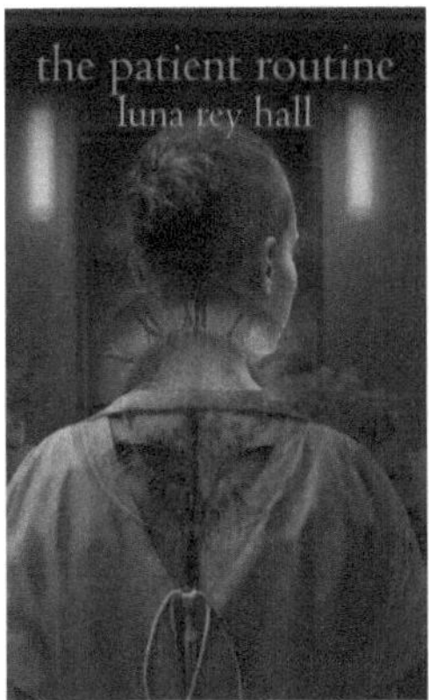

Ashton is convinced they are dying. whether it be from cancer, heart disease, or a fungal infection, they know something bad is always about to happen. after a night of health-related panic attacks, & urged by a voice in their head, Ashton decides to check in to the ER again but when another patient is brought in with an unknown ailment that puts the entire hospital on lockdown, Ashton may be trapped in their worst nightmare.

According to Dante, a **sin** is the misdirection of love-the human will, or essentially, the direction of our beings. Love the Sinner is an examination of just how those sins can kaleidoscope into **horrific** consequences creating a distorted and **deadly** landscape. These stories stand stark before you in full glaring misstep and **macabre** to show the human psyche in all its twisted reality. From grief and its rage to medical meddling to ensure a new world order to bloody **revenge** within a quantum leap, these stories seek to solidify one absolute truth: man is the scariest **monster**.

Visit our website at: www.brigidsgatepress.com